"My magic...it's gone," she told him.

Disappointment flashed across his eyes before it quickly faded. Or he masked it. *Come on, Breena, you're supposed to be good at reading people.*

He placed the barest of kisses against her mouth. "Then *tell* me stop, and I'll stop."

How could she when she ached to finally live every emotion and sensation the Osborn of her dreams had promised?

She shook her head. "I can't."

His fingers began to caress the skin below her ears, never thinking how sensitive she was there. Something dark and slightly possessive flashed across his face, turning his features stony. But this wasn't scary. Oh, it was dangerous, and should be a warning, but it was so, so tantalizing...

Breena wanted more.

Dear Reader,

Writing *Lord of Rage* was an amazing experience. Not only because I've always been a fan of dark, sizzling paranormal romance, but I also got to work with three talented authors—Gena Showalter (*Lord of the Vampires*), Jessica Andersen (*Lord of the Wolfyn*) and Nalini Singh (*Lord of the Abyss*).

We started out with a single idea—rewrite fairytales with a mystical twist —and from that, the Royal House of Shadows was born.

And, baby, did we have a blast! Our world is filled with dangerous magic, vampires and werewolves, and I couldn't resist adding one more creature to the mix—an elusive berserker possessed with a strength and rage so intense, his enemies shudder with fear. Add in a lost princess and watch as the sparks start flying.

All my best,

Jill

JILL MONROE

LORD OF RAGE

All the characters in this book have no existence outside the imagination of the author, and have no relation whatsoever to anyone bearing the same name or names. They are not even distantly inspired by any individual known or unknown to the author, and all the incidents are pure invention.

First published in Great Britain 2011
by Mills & Boon, an imprint of Harlequin (UK) Limited,
Eton House, 18-24 Paradise Road, Richmond, Surrey TW9 1SR

ISBN: 978 0 263 88333 6

089-1111

Harlequin (UK) policy is to use papers that are natural, renewable and recyclable products and made from wood grown in sustainable forests. The logging and manufacturing processes conform to the legal environmental regulations of the country of origin.

Printed in the UK
by CPI Mackays, Chatham, ME5 8TD

Jill Monroe makes her home in Oklahoma with her family. When not writing, she spends way too much time on the Internet completing "research" or updating her blog. Even when writing, she's thinking of ways to avoid cooking.

This book is dedicated to my husband and daughters—
I love you all!

Thanks so much to Gena Showalter, Jessica Andersen
and Nalini Singh—you were so much fun to work
with from beginning to end!

A special thanks goes to Tara Gavin for making it all happen.

A shout out goes to Deidre Knight, and everyone at
The Knight Agency, whose support is invaluable.

And a trip down memory lane thank you to Missi Jay who
first introduced me to berserkers back in school when we
played the game on her Atari 2600 instead of studying.

Prologue

Once upon a time, in a land unseen by human eye, there was a beautiful princess…destined to wed to further her father's political gains.

Not the kind of fairy tales Princess Breena of Elden grew up reading in the warmth of her mother's solar room. In those stories, the princesses rode glowing unicorns, slept on piles of mattresses, their rest only interrupted by a tiny pea, or lived in towering enchanted castles filled with magical creatures.

Although, none of those princesses could talk to themselves in their dreams.

As far as magical abilities, Breena's gift was pretty worthless. When she was a child, she could talk herself out of a nightmare, which was a bonus to her seven-year-old self, but now, as an adult, it didn't add anything special. Her mother could look into the dreams of men, was able to send fearful emotions into the hearts of her father's enemies or even peer into possible futures.

And once upon a time, Queen Alvina had married Breena's father for her own father's political ambition. Joining her magic to the blood drinker's power. Her oldest brother, Nicolai, could absorb the powers of others, while her other brothers Dayn and Micah could mindspeak with the blood drinkers of their kingdom.

While Breena's dream talking was not powerful…she could always connect to one particular warrior.

That's how she referred to him while awake. Warrior. As she slept, she thought of him as lover. His dark eyes matched his unruly hair that she so liked to slide her fingers through. His broad shoulders begged for her touch. Her lips. Sometimes in her dreams he'd take her in his arms, his body big and powerful, and carry her to the nearest bed. Or down to the hard floor. Sometimes it was even against the wall. Her lover would tear her clothes, ripping them from her body, then cover her skin with the softness of his lips or roughness of his callused palms.

Breena would wake up, her heart pounding and

her nipples hard and throbbing. She'd ache all over. She would draw her knees to her chest, trying to suck in air, clearing her mind of the need and the wanting.

Once she caught her breath, and her heartbeat slowed, she was left feeling only frustrated. She spent the time just after waking trying to remember. To get back into the dream. She'd been with her warrior a hundred times in her sleep, but what came after the clothes ripping and touching? Her dreams never told. Nor could she ever fully see his face. While she knew how he smelled, tasted and felt like beneath her fingertips, *he* remained elusive. Mysterious. A dream.

But one thing was for sure. If the man barged out of her dreams, through her door and stalked across her chamber, she'd be frightened. He was little more than savage. Fierce and primal. He wielded a sword as easily as she brandished a hairbrush.

Hairbrushing. Now that was important in the life of a princess. Especially one whose sole job was to marry. Breena sighed, and began to pace the confines of her room. Her feet as restless as her spirit.

And she knew those kind of thoughts would lead to danger.

In all the fairy tales her mother had read to her while growing up, a princess always got into the most trouble when she yearned for something more. She'd be tempting—no, challenging—fate, if she strode with a purpose to her window to gaze below, out past the castle gates, to the trees of the forest, and wonder…what if? What's out there? Is there anything more than this?

She might as well swing the doors open wide and invite in disaster and offer it a cup of sweet tea.

Besides, how was she prepared for adventure? Out past the gates, armed with only a few paltry magical abilities, she'd be as lost as that little boy and girl whose trail of bread crumbs was eaten by the birds. If she could defeat a fearsome ogre with a fabulous meal plan, then what lay beyond those gates might not be so worrisome. But giants and ogres wouldn't be impressed that she was competent in more than twenty kinds of dances from all over the realm. Or that she could arrange every detail from the musicians to the amount of candles needed in the great hall for a ball.

She eyed her discarded needlework. That's what a princess should be concerned about. Perfect stitches.

Tomorrow her father would begin the search for her husband. Breena knew King Aelfric had put off the task; he didn't want his daughter living away from him. His life with Alvina had started as a marriage of convenience where love had grown, and they'd forged a close-knit family. But that family was growing up and changing. Her oldest brother, Nicolai, quickly escaped the dinner table after the meal was over, most likely to the bed of a woman. As a gently bred princess of Elden, Breena wasn't supposed to know those kinds of details—but she did. Already approaching the middle of her second decade, Breena was several years older than when her mother had arrived in Elden, ready to fulfill the marriage contract.

That's why she was so restless. Their family could no longer hold back time and the changes a ticking clock brought with it. Soon she'd be leaving her childhood home, to marry, and go to another kingdom. She'd be in the arms of a man whose face she could see clearly, whose features were not fuzzy results of a dreamhaze. A man who'd show her what happened after the clothes came off. The time of her dream lover was over. It would be wrong to force him into her dreams once she belonged to another.

But she wasn't married yet. Her fingers found the timepiece her mother had given her on her fifth birthday. She wore it on a necklace around her neck, a sword and shield decorating the front.

"Why a sword?" she'd asked. Though she was more prone to running through the castle rather than walking gracefully, even her five-year-old self knew weapons of war did not suit a princess.

Her mother had shrugged, secrets darkening her green eyes. "I don't know. My magic forges the timepieces." The queen bent and kissed Breena's cheek. "But I do know it will aid you on your journey. Your destiny. Make it a good one."

A craving to see her warrior jolted her. Breena should probably be worried that those cravings hit her more and more frequently.

But if her destiny were not to be with her warrior, then she'd take her mother's advice and make her journey a good one. Breena kicked off her delicate slippers and lay down on her soft mattress, not bothering to slip out of her dress or tug the covers up over her chin. She closed her eyes and pictured a door. When her mother tried to teach her how to take over the dreamworld, she'd told her that all she had to do was turn the knob, and walk through. The door would take her anywhere she wished to be.

The door only took her to the mind of her fierce lover, and right now that was the only place she wanted to go.

She found him sharpening the steel of his blade. Breena often found him taking care of his weapons. In her dreams, she was never made nervous by his axes or swords or knives. She relished his ferocity, his ability to protect. Attack. She leaned against a tree and simply watched the play of his muscles across his shirtless back as he slid the cloth around the hilt.

Breena never found much time to simply observe him. The warrior in him was always on alert, and because she was in a dream, his features were never clearly defined. Did lines from his eyes indicate he liked to laugh? Were there lines across his forehead, marking him as a man of intensity and concentration? All she could see were broad brushstrokes. Not the kinds of things that would tell her who he was inside.

A smile curved her lips when his shoulders tensed. Her lover had sensed her presence. The sword and cleaning cloth dropped to the grass at his feet as he turned. Her nipples hardened as his gaze traveled up and down her body, his breath little more than a hiss. Breena squinted, once more trying to peer through the dreamhaze that never seemed to let her see the true angles of his face. Only his eyes. Those intense brown eyes.

His footsteps were silent as he walked over the leaves and twigs carpeting the ground. She pushed away from the tree, moving toward him, wanting to meet her lover as quickly as she could now that he knew she'd arrived.

This would be their last time together.

Or at least it should. She should be focusing on her kingdom, and aiding her father in selecting her husband.

Breena twined her hands around her lover's neck to bring his lips down to hers. The man in her dream never kissed her gently, as she suspected a courtier bred to rule over a castle would. No, this man's lips were demanding. His kiss was passionate and filled with primal desire.

"I want you naked," he told her, his voice tight.

She blinked at him, startled for a moment. He had never talked before in her dreams. Breena liked his voice, elemental and filled with hunger for her. He reached for the material at her shoulders, ready to tear, but she stilled his hand. She didn't want him to be the seducer this day, not that his lovemaking would be considered a smooth seduction. No, she wanted to be equal partners this last time. Breena wanted to undress for him.

With a twist of her wrists, she tugged at the ribbon between her shoulder blades and felt the fabric of her bodice give. Propelled by a slow roll of her shoulders, her dress began to fall. His eyes narrowed when her breasts were revealed, her nipples growing even tighter before his eyes. He reached for her. Breena knew what he would do the moment he had her in his grasp, and she laughed.

"Not yet," she teased. Then she picked up her skirts and ran to the tree. She'd never played this game before…never thought to. She knew on some level her warrior lover would savor the chase. He would win, but she had every intention of letting him find her.

Although her lover was silent, Breena sensed he was close. She laughed again when his hand curved around her waist. He tugged her back against the solidness of his chest. The hard ridge of him pressed against her, and something needy and achy made her stomach feel hollow. The urge to tease and run vanished in an instant. Breena wanted—no, she *needed*—his hands on her body and his lips on her breasts.

Something hard clamped across her mouth. Confusion filled his dark eyes and the solid lines of him began to blur. Fade. His hands tightened around her arms, but it was too late.

"Stay with me," he demanded. "What's happening to you?"

She struggled, willing herself farther through the doorway, closer to him. But it was too late.

Breena fought against the force holding her head in place.

"Quiet," a voice ordered.

She shook her head, and reached for her lover's hand. But she grasped only air. Some thing, some force, was taking her away from him. "Help me," she tried to call, but the hand covering her mouth wouldn't let her speak.

And he was gone.

Breena was back in her bedchamber. Rolfe, a

member of her parents' personal security, stood over her. "Quiet, princess. The castle's under attack. They've already taken the king and queen."

She sat up, the last vestiges of her dream fading completely. As the meaning behind the guard's words sank in, her fingers began to chill and her heart began to race. "We must help them," she whispered.

Rolfe shook his head. "It's too late for them. They'd want me to get you and your brothers and take you through the secret passageway out of the castle."

"But..." she began to protest. Tears filmed her eyes and her throat began to tighten. The passageway had been built by some long-ago ancestor as a last-resort escape route if the inhabitants of the castle feared there was no other option but flight.

"Come, princess, and hurry. Put on some shoes. We must fetch Micah and Dayn."

"What about Nicolai?"

The guard shook his head.

Fear slammed into her. The enormity of their danger finally penetrated her dreamhaze. This wasn't an attack on the castle, like those easily repelled in the past; this was an all-out onslaught. "He's been taken, too?"

"I cannot find him. Come, we must save who we can."

Breena began to shudder, but took a deep breath.

She had to be strong and face whatever danger lay ahead. Her brothers depended on her.

After sliding her feet into the slippers at the foot of her bed, she followed Rolfe down the hallway that led her to Dayn's and Micah's chambers. Below she heard the clash and clang of sword against shield. The war cry. And the sound of death.

She quickened her pace, quietly stealing into Micah's room first as Rolfe went to Dayn's. Earlier they'd celebrated Micah's fifth birthday. It was now up to her to make sure he celebrated another. If she had her mother's abilities, she'd already be placing awakening thoughts in her brother's dreams. Instead, she would have to gently shake him on the shoulder.

"Where's my brother?" she asked the maid after walking into the chamber where her brother slept.

"His nanny took him. To one of the high rooms in the castle."

Breena sagged in relief.

"But what should we do about the little cousin?"

Her hand flew to cover her gasp. Their cousin, Gavin, who wasn't much older than four, had come for the party. She doubted any of the guards would think to check on him. She raced down the hallway to where he slept.

"Gavin, darling," she whispered. "Get dressed. You've got to come with me and Rolfe."

Her little cousin rubbed at his eyes. "Why?" he asked, more asleep than awake.

"We're playing hide-and-seek," she told him with a smile.

He sat up in bed, confused by the timing, but still ready for the game. Gavin was young enough for her to carry. She simply lifted him from the covers and draped him over her shoulder. She sang a soft lullaby in his ear so he wouldn't grow fretful and loud.

Rolfe joined her in the hallway. "Dayn's not in his room."

Fear for her dear older brother made her shake all over again. "Perhaps he's already escaped."

Doubt flickered in Rolfe's eyes for a moment, before the guard quickly masked it. Dayn was in charge of protecting the outer walls of the castle. Of course he'd be involved in any kind of defense. But their defenses had already been breached. That would mean her brother—

No, she would not allow her thoughts to go there. Right now she must take care of Gavin. Rolfe was already rushing toward the corridor that would lead to the escape route no one in Elden had needed in several generations. Who would be attacking them? Why? Their kingdom had been at peace with most every other in the realm.

Rolfe pushed aside a heavy tapestry revealing the door leading to their means of escape. The sounds of fighting still echoed from below, but were growing closer. The hidden door groaned when Rolfe pushed at the ancient wood. When it finally gave way, the hinges objected loudly after their lack of use for years.

"Stop!"

Breena turned to see a hideous creature, one created from evil. Its eight legs, gleaming with razors and dripping with the blood of her people, sped toward her. It would get them all if she didn't do something to distract it.

"You must walk now, Gavin."

"But I want you to carry me," he protested.

"Princess," the monster called to her, baring its fangs. She realized the revolting beast was focused solely on her. Would do anything to get her, including killing her cousin.

"Go!" she screamed, pushing Gavin into Rolfe's side, and slammed the door shut.

"Breena," she heard her little cousin cry. But then she heard a comforting click as Rolfe slid the dead bolt from the inside. Relief made her legs shake. Taking a deep breath, she turned. The monster was almost at her side. Like her mother, this creature wielded magic, except it harnessed the dark powers that came only from corrupting life-sustaining blood.

It shoved her against the wall, one of its razor-adorned legs trapping her in place. It tugged at the handle, but the door didn't budge. "No matter. They can't hide in there forever." Then it looked over at her. Its eyes were cold. She'd never seen eyes so full of…nothingness. It chilled her.

A smile, if one could even call it that, pulled at its upper lip. "Come. The master will want to see you."

It grabbed her arm, and she sucked in a breath as one of the razors pierced her skin. Her captor dragged her to the staircase where the fighting still waged. Only the crash of sword against sword was already fading as it pulled her down to the great hall. The agonized moans of the injured and dying mingled with the terrified weeping of the captured. Then she spotted her parents on the dais where they held court, chained to their thrones. A mocking humiliation.

Anger began to grow in her chest, chasing away the fear. Her father lay slumped where he once ruled proudly. Blood ran down his cheek and pooled at his feet. So much blood. Too much blood. A sob tore from her throat, and she yanked her arm from her captor's grasp. She couldn't let him die like that. Not her father, who ruled with justice, who loved his people.

The blow came from behind. It knocked her to the floor, the cold stone of the hearth cutting her forehead. Blackness began to move across her vision, and she blinked to try to clear it and the pain. She met her father's gaze. He didn't have much longer to live. Breena forced herself to look at her mother. Her beautiful mother with the striking silver hair, now stained red from the blood she'd shed.

Her parents reached for each other, and the gesture comforted her. They'd die together. Dark brown eyes flashed across her mind. Her dream warrior would fight these creatures who practiced blood magic. He'd die trying to save, to avenge. She wished he were here now.

"No!" called a man, his tone cold. He had a voice that sounded like death.

Breena knew without having to be told that the man, or something that had once been a man, who raced toward her parents was the Blood Sorcerer. A legend. A rumor. Tall and skeletal, this was the creature mothers warned of; he took those foolish to leave the safety of Elden and turned them evil.

Something potent swirled between her parents' outstretched hands. They weren't reaching for each other as she'd first thought, they were rallying their powers. Breena reached for the timepiece, her fingers worrying into the sword and shield decorating the front. How ironic, when what she really needed *was* a sword and shield.

And a man who could wield that sword.

Her timepiece began to warm and glow against her skin. A wave of magic shuddered through her entire body, and Breena no longer felt the sting from the cut of her temple or the coldness of the hard stone beneath her body.

Breena's last thought was of her warrior.

Chapter 1

A furore libera nos, Domine!
Deliver us from the fury, O Lord!

Ten Years Ago

Osborn's fingers tightened around the smooth handle of his spear. He'd spent countless hours peeling away the bark and sanding the rough wood until it felt easy in his hand. His legs shook in anticipation as he sat at the campfire, watching the logs turn orange and the smoke rise to the stars.

His last night as a child.

Tomorrow he'd follow the path his father—and his father's father and the generations of his forebearers—had once all walked since the beginning of the beginning. Tomorrow he'd meet the final challenge. Tomorrow he'd become a man or he'd die.

"You must sleep," his father told him.

Osborn glanced up. Even in the dimness of the firelight he could recognize the tension bracketing his father's eyes. Tomorrow he'd either join his father as a warrior or his father would be burying another son.

"I'm not tired," he admitted.

With a nod, his father joined him on the ground, the fire warming the chill night air. "Neither could I that night."

Osborn's eyes narrowed. Even though he'd asked a dozen times about his father's Bärenjagd, he'd said little. A father's task was to prepare his son for the fight, but what to expect, how to feel… that battle was left for each boy to face alone. On his own terms. It defined the warrior he'd become.

If he lived.

An abrupt shake to his shoulder awoke Osborn in the morning. Somehow he'd fallen into a deep sleep. "It's time."

The fire had died, and he resisted the urge to pull his pelt around him tighter. Then he remembered.

It was *now*.

A smile tugged at his father's lower lip when he

saw the suddenness of Osborn's actions. In a flash of movement he was dressed, bedroll secured and spear in hand.

"It's time," he announced to his father, repeating the words he'd been given.

They were eye-to-eye now, and still Osborn would grow taller. Later tonight he'd be returning a man, welcomed to take his place among the warriors.

His father nodded. "I will tell you what my father told me, and I suspect his father and the fathers before him. What you must do now, you do alone. Leave your aleskin here, and take no food. Nothing but your weapon. Be brave, but above all, be honorable."

"How will you know when it is done?" he asked.

"I will know. Now go."

Osborne turned on his heel, and trekked silently though the brush as his father had first taught him so many years ago. One of his many lessons. Last night they'd slept on the outskirts of the sacred bear lands. Now was the time he must cross over.

With a deep breath he stepped onto the sacred land, reveling in the unexpected thrust of power that pounded into his body. The surge swelled in his chest, then grew, infusing his limbs, his fingers. With new energy, he gripped his spear and began to run. Running faster than he'd ever run before, he followed that tug of power, trusting his instincts.

Time lost meaning as he ran. He never grew tired, even as the sun continued to rise in the sky. His vision narrowed, and the heavy tang of musk scented the air. Bear musk.

The time was *now.*

Every muscle, every sense, tightened. Instinct again told him to turn his head, and then he saw it.

The bear was a giant. Towering more than two feet above Osborn, its fierce claws curved, its dark brown fur pulled tight over taut muscles. Osborn met the fearsome creature's eyes. Again something powerful slammed into him, and his muscles locked. His body froze.

The bear growled at him, a thunderous sound that made the earth beneath his feet rumble. Osborn felt his eyes widen, but he still could not move.

The time was *now.*

Osborn forced his fingers to shift, his arm to relax. Then, with a flowing arc he'd practiced alongside his father hundreds of times, he sent his spear soaring. The sound of its sharpened tip whizzed through the air. The animal roared when Osborn's weapon sank into his chest. Blood darkened its coat.

With a guttural cry, Osborn sprinted to where the

bear had stumbled to the ground, pawing at the wood lodged inside its body. The animal went wild as Osborn neared, striking toward him with those killer claws. A wave of fear shuddered down his spine. The rusty, salty scent of blood hit his nostrils. The breathy, angered groaning of the bear made Osborn shake his head, trying to clear the sound. The bear rolled to its feet, once more towering above him, and close. So close.

He steeled his resolve. He was to be a warrior. A brave one. Osborn reached for the spear. One weapon was all a boy was allowed to take. The bear swiped at him, his claws ripping through the cloth of his shirt, tearing the skin of his bicep. With a mighty blow, the animal sent Osborn to the ground, the air knocked out of his lungs by the force.

Forget the pain. Forget the blood. Forget the fear.

Once again, Osborn's focus narrowed. He reached for the spear again, this time dragging it from the bear's body. But not without a price. The mighty animal clawed at him again, leaving a trail of torn flesh crossing from his shoulder down to his hip. The pain was agony, and his vision blurred, but he steadied his hand and aimed at the animal's throat.

The animal fell to the ground again, but Osborn knew it would not be getting back to its feet. He met those dark brown eyes of the bear. A wave of anguished compassion settled into Osborn. *This* was why the warriors never told of their experiences.

The bear took a labored breath, blood trickling from its nose. Osborn squeezed his eyes tight, fighting the nausea that threatened. His glance drifted to the pain-glazed eyes of the bear. He was dishonoring this great animal's spirit by letting it suffer. The bear's soul clamored for its release. Its next journey.

The time was *now.*

Osborn grabbed the spear once more, then plunged it directly in the bear's heart, ending its life. A rush of energy slammed into him, almost knocking him backward. He fought it, but it was ripping and tearing through his soul. The *ber* energy fused with his own nature, turning him into the warrior the rest of the realm referred to as *berserkers.*

He felt his muscle begin to quiver, feeling weak from his loss of blood. But the wounds would heal. He'd be stronger than ever before. Osborn gulped in air and stumbled his way back to the place where he'd parted from his father.

Intense relief passed across his father's face, and his brown eyes warmed when he saw Osborn approach. Osborn immediately straightened despite the pain. He was a warrior; he'd greet his father that way. But his father hugged him, grabbed him and held him tight to his chest. For a few moments he basked in his father's pride and love before his father broke away and began packing away their camp supplies.

"It was harder than I thought. I didn't think I'd feel this way," Osborn blurted out for no reason he could guess. He regretted his rash words instantly. That was a boy's sentiments. Not a man's. Not a warrior's.

But his father only nodded. "It's not supposed to be easy. Taking of a life, any life, should never be something done without need and compassion." He stood, slinging his pack over his shoulder. "Guide me to the bear. We must prepare it."

They trekked silently together, crossing into the sacred land to where the bear had taken its final breaths. His father taught him to honor the bear in the ancient ways, then they set to work.

"Now you possess the heart of the bear. As a warrior of Ursa, you will carry the bear's spirit with you. Your *ber* spirit will always be there, waiting silent within you, ready for your call. The strength of the bear comes to you when you wear your Bärenhaut," his father told him, lifting up the bear pelt. "Do not don your pelt without thought and careful consideration. You will be able to kill, Osborn, and kill easily. But only with honor."

"I will, Father," he vowed with a humble sense of pride. "What do we do now?"

"We take the meat back so our people can eat. The claws we use for our weapons. We don't waste what the bear has given us. We revere its sacrifice." His father ran a finger down the bear's fur. "But the pelt, that belongs to you. You wear it only when you go into battle and must call upon the spirit of the bear."

As he'd observed with his father, and the dozen of Ursa warriors who guarded their homeland. Now he was joining their elite ranks.

They came at night. But then vampires were strongest at night. Attacking when all would be asleep. While the warriors and their sons were on Bärenjagd. A coward's choice.

The cries of women filled the night air. The blaze of burned homes and barns and grain silos lit up the sky. Father and son took in the scene below. Osborn's mother was down there. His sister.

His father shucked his clothing, grabbing for his Bärenhaut and sword, which were never far out of reach. Osborn's own bear pelt wasn't ready, not yet dried by the sun, but still he reached for the fur, drawing it about his bare shoulders. Blood and sinew still clung to the pelt, and seeped into Osborn through the wounds on his arm and down his body. A powerful rage took him over. He felt nothing else. No sadness over the bear, no worry or concern for his brothers or sister and mother, no anguish over the loss of the food stores that would keep his people alive through the harsh winter. Osborn felt nothing but the killing rage.

With a war cry, he charged down the hill, to his village, his people. To do battle. Not heeding the warning of his father. A vampire turned at his call, blood dripping from his chin, a chilling smile on his cruel lips.

The anger, the force of his rage, overpowered him. He charged the vamp, grabbing for his throat, tearing at his flesh, ripping at the creature's body with his bare hands. He didn't need a stake, only his fist, slamming through skin, bone, to the heart below. The vamp collapsed at his feet.

Osborn turned, ready to kill another. And he did. Again and again. But the Ursa warriors were outnumbered. Armed with clubs, the vampires waited to ambush the father-and-son pairs slowly returning, easy and unaware targets. The creatures knew what they were doing, fighting his people with neither blade nor fire.

The bodies of his neighbors lay among the blood drinkers he'd killed. In the distance, he still saw his father in the fight, easily taking on two vamps, his berserkergang a trusted ally. But then he saw his father fall. Vamps were ready to suck the last of his life force. His spirit.

"No," he cried, his rage growing, building. He

grabbed a sword from one of the fallen vamps as he ran. The blade might not do damage to his flesh, but it would soon find a home in a vampire's bitter, dark heart.

The blood drinker at his father's throat lost his head without knowing the threat approaching. The second vampire was able to put up a fight, fueling Osborn's anger. He laughed into the dawn as the vampire fell at his feet. He turned ready for more, to kill more. His rage only soothed by the death of his enemy. But he was surrounded.

Vampires moved at incredible speeds to join those slowly encircling him. Even with his berserkergang upon him, the spirit of the bear filling him, he knew he could not defeat this many vampires. The vampires had made sure there was no one to help him.

He'd just make sure he took as many as he could with them when he died. He raised his sword, preparing to do battle.

Just as quickly as the vampires had moved to surround him, they stopped. Light began to filter through the leaves of the trees. One by one the vampires left, faster than his eyes could track.

"Come back and fight," he called to them.

The sound of the wind rustling over the grass was his only answer.

"Fight, cowards."

But his rage was fading, only anguish left in its place. His pelt began to slip off his shoulders.

Those vampires still left dying on the ground began to sizzle. Smoke rose to the sky from their bodies, and soon they were nothing but ash. The smell was horrific, and he turned away, sinking to the ground by his father's prone body.

He lifted his father's hand. It was cold, lifeless. Tears pricked at his eyes, but he blinked them back, in honor of the spirit of the man who'd died to save his people.

The vamp Osborn had relieved of his head left nothing behind but his tunic. Under the cover of the night, he hadn't realized the attackers had been similarly dressed. His own people did not dress alike when they engaged in battle. But one kingdom of the realm did. The magical vampires of Elden. He recognized the navy and purple colors of Elden's royal military guard.

It made no sense. Nothing made sense. There'd been peace between his people and Elden for generations. The king only had to ask, and the Ursan warriors would fight at his side.

Only one thing made sense in Osborn's mind—every last resident of Elden would die by his hand.

The day was filled with hard, gruesome work. He carefully gathered the bodies of his people, trying to remember them as they were—his neighbors, his school buddies, not these lifeless bodies covered in blood and desecrated by bloodthirsty vampires. He found his mother cradling the small, lifeless body of his sister, protecting her even in death. His sister's favorite bear doll in its frilly pink dress lay nearby. Trampled.

By the time the sun was overhead, his grisly task was nearly complete. Tradition dictated the funeral pyre should be set at dusk, burning into the night. But he suspected his family would forgive him for not making himself an easy target for vampires waiting to rip out his throat. Except there were two members of his family unaccounted for. His two younger brothers, Bernt and Torben.

For the first time since his berserkergang left him, and he was free to see the carnage left in Elden's wake, did Osborn feel a small twinge of hope. His younger brothers played marathon games of hide-and-seek, but this time their skill at not being found might have saved their lives. And their older brother knew their favorite place. Picking up his steel and pelt, Osborn took off at a sprint.

The earthen smells of the cave was a welcome relief from the smoky ash and blood and death where he'd been working. He whistled into the cave. He heard no returning sound, but he sensed they were in there. Wanted them to be. Needed it. Osborn had never understood his younger siblings' fascination for this place. He hated the enclosed, dark hole that was the cave, but after chores, his brothers would spend hours in the shelter of the rock. He hoped it held true this time. Osborn took a step inside. "Bernt, are you here? Torben? Come out, brothers," he urged quietly.

He heard the quick intake of breath, and a relief like no other made his throat tighten.

"It's Osborn. Take my hand," he suggested as he forced his fingers deeper into the cave with dread and hope.

He was rewarded by small fingers encircling his hand. Two sets of hands. Thank the gods.

He gently drew them outside the cave, their dirty faces blinking in the harsh sunlight so welcome.

"Mom told us to hide," Bernt said, guilt already hardening his young face.

"We wanted to fight," Torben defended. "But she made us promise."

He gave a quick squeeze to each of their shoulders. The way his father would. "You did the right thing. Now you will live to fight another day." As he had lived. As he would fight.

After gathering what stores they could find and carry, his brothers helped Osborn light the pyre, saying a prayer for the spirits of their people.

The three of them traveled far away from Ursa, crossing through the various kingdoms of their world. Osborn spent his days hustling for food, trying to keep his brothers safe and work on their training. But he soon learned the only marketable skills a warrior of Ursa possessed was for that of killing. Hired out as a mercenary. An assassin.

The boy who'd once mourned the death of a fearless animal now enjoyed the killing. The smell of death. The pleas of his prey.

Osborn thrived under the threat of his imminent death. Not even the pleasure found between a woman's legs could quell the blood fury. Only when he faced the steel of another's blade did his senses awake. Only when the sting of pain lashed through him did he feel…anything.

Only when he witnessed his life's blood pumping from his body with each beat of his heart did he hear the echoing pulse of his ancestors'. Now gone. All dead. Except him. He always survived.

But the royals of the various kingdoms of their realm grew worried and fearful of this man they'd once hired. A man who took jobs without question was not a man to be trusted.

Now he was the hunted.

And once again, eight years since fleeing his homeland, Osborn gathered his younger brothers and fled, this time deep into the woody plains of the sacred bear, a place where no one but an Ursa warrior would dare to tread. And those warriors were all gone.

Chapter 2

Breena stumbled through the tall grass and bramble. Large thorns tore at the delicate skin of her bare legs, but she no longer cried out in pain. If she were at home in Elden, she could blunt the pain with her magic, force it through some door in her mind and slam it shut. But that power eluded her in this unfamiliar place. Here, wherever she was, she had to endure it. Push through the throbbing of her tired muscles and the sting from the cuts and abrasions running up and down her arms and legs.

The voluminous folds of her once-ornate skirt, her protection from the harsh wilderness, was now gone, ripped and torn away as she'd traveled. Blood ran down her legs from the scratches, joining the dried layer already caked to her calves. Her knees were skinned, and still she drove herself to put one foot in front of another. She pushed forward as she'd been doing since she'd been ripped from her own realm and thrown…somewhere.

She stepped on a rock, its sharp edge digging into the tender arch of her foot; the dainty slippers she'd been wearing when she'd woken up were long gone. She stumbled again, this time falling to the ground, and, as she landed, she lost the last of her strength. Breena would cry if she had even a tiny sliver of energy. She hadn't eaten in days, the only water she'd had was when she'd sipped off plant leaves. No one looking at her now would ever think she'd once been a princess. One who could do magic.

She pulled her hands together, closed her eyes and concentrated, willing her magic to appear. Produce a trickle of water or a berry to eat. But it did not. Just like it hadn't appeared since she'd arrived with only two thoughts she couldn't chase from her mind. Two seemingly opposing goals.

To survive. To kill.

Breena rubbed at her brows, trying to soothe the sharp ache knotting behind her eyes. Those goals seemed to come from someplace outside of her. Survival from someone warm, caring… Her mother? She hugged her arms around herself—yes, her mother would want her to live.

To avenge. To kill. That thought was masculine. Powerful. Authoritative. Her father.

And yet, she'd not do either. She'd neither live nor live to kill. Unless killing herself by pushing forward counted.

She doubted it was what her father had in mind. Her fingers went to the timepiece that had somehow survived whatever kind of hellish force brought her to this wild place. An unknown vengeance burned deep inside her, and she understood, perhaps since waking up dazed and alone in this strange land, that her parents had done something to her. Why here? Were they de— Pain ripped behind her eyes, making her gasp. Her parents… The throbbing always came when her thoughts lingered too long on them. She didn't even know if they were alive or dead. But each time her attention drifted their way, Breena could see a little more. Until the pain took over.

Breena would die either way, so she might as well keep going.

Bracing for the pain, she pulled herself up off the ground and stood. She took an unsteady step, followed by another.

A bird flew overhead. She'd heard a story once about a lost boy following a bird and it leading him to a beautiful meadow filled with fruit and a pond of cool, delicious water. Of course, the boy got lost there, and never returned home. Breena was sure there was some lesson buried in the story, warning curious children about wandering off, but right now, she could only focus on the drinking and eating part.

Shading her eyes, she decided following the bird was the best plan she had so far. She spotted another skull attached to a tree. This was the third she'd seen just like that.

A bear skull.

She had to be in Ursa. The clan with the affinity to the great bear. Fought like them, she'd heard her father comment, clearly impressed. The Ursan kingdom had been allied to her own since her great-grandfather's time. He'd negotiated the conditions himself. If she could just find them, find their village, perhaps they could help her get back to Elden. No, the Ursans were all gone. If only those warriors could help her with both goals, live and kill. The thoughts she'd woken up with two days ago.

Was it two? Felt like more. Like her home in Elden was a lifetime ago. Time was so hazy. It didn't make sense. Like so many things since she'd woken up. Breena remembered something happening to her home, fear for her brothers. When she closed her eyes tight, images of her mother and father appeared. Performing last magic.

But why did they send her here?

Pain ripped across her chest, and Breena shook

her head. She didn't want those images in her mind. But something had happened to her. Traces of magic surrounded her. Someone else's magic. Certainly not hers.

Instead, she tried to replace the images of her parents with that of her warrior. As she slept beneath the protective cover of trees, Breena attempted to walk into his dream. His mind. But just like her missing magic, her warrior was lost to her now, too. She found no door.

So she followed the bird, a hawk, as it made a lazy loop in the sky above her head.

"Please be thirsty," she whispered. *And hungry.*

The bird made a squealing sound and dove. Breena forced energy into her feet. Her legs. Not her misplaced magic, but old-fashioned willpower. She sprinted as she chased the bird. Jumping over a fallen log, avoiding a thorny bush.

She came into a small clearing, only to spy the bird claiming a perch rather than hunting for sustenance. Disappointment cut into her side like a stitch, and she rested her hands on her thighs, dragging in large gulps of air. No meadow, no pond… just a perch. She glanced up to glare at the hawk, and then realized it was perched upon the gable of a cottage. A well-kept cottage.

The clearing around the wood cabin was neat and free of weeds and stones. A small plowed area—a garden, perhaps—lay to one side. That meant there had to be water and food inside.

With a squeal she raced to the door, fearing it would be locked. But she'd break through the window if she had to. She knocked on the door, but no one came to invite her inside. Polite niceties of etiquette over, she turned the handle, and thankfully the knob twisted easily and she pushed the door open.

Wholesome grain and cinnamon scented the air. There, on the stove, stood a large pot of oatmeal. Everything in her body seized. Food. Food. Reaching for the ladle she began to eat from the large utensil. Irritated with the awkwardness of it all, she tossed the spoon on the counter and dug in with her hands, feeding herself like an animal. Her mother would be appalled.

But then it was her mother who'd wanted her to survive. To live.

Her very empty stomach protested as the food hit, and she forced herself to slow down. Breena didn't want to make herself sick. A pitcher stood on the table. She didn't care what was inside; even if it were blackberry juice, she was going to drink it. She put the spout to her lips, and allowed the sweet taste of lemonade to fill her mouth and slide down her throat.

Despite her efforts to slow down, nausea struck her and she began to shudder. She took a blind step to the left, falling down hard on a chair at an awkward angle. With a sharp crack, the legs gave way and the chair broke, taking her to the floor.

Breena began to laugh. Tears formed at the corners of her eyes and fell down her cheeks. She'd found herself a cottage, and she was still stumbling to the ground. No one would believe her to be a princess with oatmeal drying on her hands and lemonade dripping down her chin.

The wave of nausea passed only to be replaced by a bone-deep weariness. Breena had already eaten this family's meal and broken their furniture, but she didn't think she could attempt another thing except lay her head down and close her eyes. She spotted an open door leading to another room of the cottage. Her spirits lifted; perhaps a bed awaited. With one last surge of strength, she crawled across the wooden floor, delighted to see not one but three beds. None were as grand or ornate as the sleigh bed she had in her tower room in Elden. No heavy draperies hung from hooks above the headboard, nor was the bed covered by mounds and mounds of fluffy pillows in bright colors, but they were flat, clean and looked comfortable. Of course, anything would be comfortable after sleeping on the hard, cold ground for days...weeks? Her perception was off; she couldn't grasp what was real.

What she needed was a good night's sleep. She

should leave some kind of a note for the inhabitants, but her eyes were already drooping. The combination of fear, hunger, weakness and displacement finally zapped what was left of her waning strength. She fell across the largest of the beds, too tired to even slip beneath the covers.

Too weary to even attempt dreamtime with the warrior.

It was a good thing they weren't hunting for food because his brothers' loud voices would have scared away any game. Osborn glanced over at Bernt. In a year, he'd be looking him in the eye. Torben wasn't that far behind.

If they still lived in their homeland and he was any kind of good big brother, Bernt would have already tested his strengths as a warrior at his Bärenjagd by now. Guilt slammed into Osborn. He should have prepared his brother better, led him to the rites that would make him a man before his people. Before all of the Ursa realm.

But there was no Ursa realm anymore.

What good was the Bärenjagd, the berserkergang, if he couldn't save his people? If it left him hunted like an animal? Nothing better than another man's mercenary?

Yet a restlessness hovered over his brother. A need not fulfilled. Bernt had become prone to taking off into the woods, with dark moods and fits of anger that didn't resemble the avenging rage of a berserker.

Unfulfilled destiny.

Osborn would have to do something. And soon. An urgency now laced the air. Doubt after doubt crashed into him. Had he worked with Bernt enough on handling his spear? Keeping his balance in combat? Steadying his nerves?

Osborn scrubbed his hand down his face. More than likely, his thoughts mirrored the worries and reservations of his own father. Thoughts his father must have hidden as he'd stared into the fire while his young son Osborn slept nearby.

Only Osborn wasn't Bernt's father. Didn't possess his wisdom. What could he teach about honor? He'd lost his years ago.

His brothers zipped past him, racing for the door. Bernt was in a good mood today. A rarity. Chopping wood for hours under the blazing sun had bled the aggression from him. For the day. The two crashed through the front door, knocking off each other's hats, and generally being loud. But then when were they not loud? At least he'd given them a childhood of carefree days. At least he'd given them that much.

The pot of oatmeal he'd thought he'd left on the stove now lay on the kitchen table. The ladle lay discarded on the scarred wooden countertop, slops of grain sliding down the sides and waiting to be cleaned.

"Who did that?" he bellowed.

The lemonade pitcher was filthy. Dried glops of oatmeal stuck to the handle and it appeared someone had taken a drink directly from the spout.

"No one's going to want to drink from this now. How hard is it to get a cup?"

And when had he become an old woman?

"I didn't do it," Torben said.

"Me neither," Bernt replied. Already his shoulders were stiffening, his brighter mood growing stormy.

"I don't care who did it." How many times had he said that since taking over the care and responsibility of his younger brothers? "Both of you can help clean it up." And that?

Osborn moved, and the sound of splintering wood broke the tense silence. "Look at the chair." He pointed to the remnants of Bernt's attempt at furniture.

"There's another one that's busted," Bernt grumbled.

"You'll get the hang of woodworking," Osborn told him, forcing as much reassurance into his voice as he could muster.

Bernt's look grew defiant. "I'm supposed to be a warrior."

Yes, and there lay the problem.

"Well, now you're a would-be warrior who works with wood," he said simply, as if it fixed and explained everything. But how long could the three of them pretend?

Torben crouched and reached for one of the busted chair legs. He tossed it from hand to hand as Osborn had once done with a spear. Osborn had been ignoring the fact that his other brother also exhibited every sign of being a warrior.

"This chair didn't fall apart by itself. It broke with force." His brother met his gaze. "Someone's been here."

"Told you I didn't make the mess," Bernt said, his voice still a mix of defiance and triumph. "Someone's been eating our food."

"And someone's been sitting in our chair," echoed his brother.

But Osborn barely heard. All his senses were focusing. Narrowing. The cold began to creep down his limbs, hardening his muscles. For the first time he noticed the tiny bits of grass leading to their bedchamber.

His fingers slid down his boot for the blade. His brother was already handing him the pack sheltering his berserker pelt. The pack was always within reaching distance of one of them.

He crept silently across the wooden floor. Telling his brothers to stay back would be useless. Someone had invaded their home. Any warning

Osborn issued to them could not compete with Ursan warrior instincts.

A soft sound, like a moan, drifted from the bedchamber. The chill began to subside. His berserkergang sensed whatever made that noise was no threat, and began to stand down. But that moan… it shafted through his body, alerting all his senses in a different manner. As a man.

The three of them peered inside the room.

"Someone's sleeping in your bed. And she's still there."

Osborn stalked into the room. The woman lay on her stomach on his bed, her long blond hair fanning across his pillow. Something primal kicked him in the gut.

"Is she dead?" Torben whispered.

His gaze lowered to the even rise and fall of her back. He shook his head, relief chasing the last of his berserker's nature away. "She's asleep."

Why were they whispering? This woman had invaded their home, messed his kitchen and destroyed his property. But he couldn't work up any sense of outrage.

The woman looked as if she'd fallen onto his bed, and gone to sleep. Like a dream come true for most men.

She sighed, a soft delicate sound, and hiked up her leg. No covers hid her from his view. Her legs were bare, and his gaze followed all the way up.

Holy hell. What was left of her skirt has been ripped away, and he could see the rounded curve of her ass. Desire, hot and heavy, hit him. Hardened him. Sweat broke out along his brow.

He forced his eyes downward once more, this time noticing the deep cuts and abrasions all up and down her legs, marring her delicate skin.

How did—? Who would—?

Something deeply buried rose within him. A force as strong as his bear spirit. Not warring, but mingling. Joining and growing more powerful. *His.*

"Leave," he ordered his brothers.

Neither needed a second command from Osborn. They recognized the chill in his voice. The forces charging through him. They fairly tripped over each other fleeing the room.

A line crossed her brow as the clumsy shuffling footsteps of his brothers escaping the bedroom penetrated her sleep. She rolled over and his gaze traveled down once more. He'd never seen a face so delicate, her bones fine and skin that looked almost too soft to touch. Her chin was another thing—not softly rounded like the rest of her, but stubborn. The flaw only made her more appealing. Pink tipped her cheeks and nose, like someone who'd been in the sun too long. The material of her bodice was dirty and torn, many parts missing, but Osborn could tell it had once been fine. Expensive.

Who was she?

The woman took a deep breath, her breasts rising and drawing his attention. Osborn could not look away. Flashes of her bare skin peeked through the rips of her clothing. His eyes narrowed and he could see the rosier skin of her nipples.

His.

The primal conviction drove a harsh thrust of heat and desire through him. Osborn stepped toward her. Peered down at her sleeping figure in his bed. He could see every line of her face. The dark fan of her eyelashes. The soft curve of her bottom lip. He forced his hands down to his sides. Fisted his hands so he wouldn't be tempted to touch her. Trace his fingers along the skin of her arm. Her cheek. Find out for himself if she was as soft as she looked.

What the hell was he thinking? She wasn't his. One person didn't possess another. He willed his body to back down.

Just then her eyes opened, green and sleepy. His gaze darted to her lips, which were turning into a smile. A smile for him.

"Warrior," she said, and hugged his pillow to her chest, still more asleep than awake.

Everything in him controlled and restrained disappeared. Osborn needed to feel her in his arms, kiss that mouth. He reached for her shoulders, dragging her unresisting body toward him. Her eyes widened as he dipped his head.

He tasted the sweet tartness of the lemonade on her lips. But nothing in this world he'd ever sampled was as good as her. Osborn wound his fingers in the messy strands of her blond hair, drawing her still closer. Smashing the softness of her breasts against his chest.

His heartbeat pounded, and he took advantage of her unresisting lips and plunged his tongue in her mouth, savoring her, twining his tongue with hers. No, nothing he'd ever had tasted this good. Felt this good. Made him feel this good. Except…

Except one thing. The woman who invaded his dreams. Tormented his nights. Left him alone feeling tortured, battling a fierce wanting and hungry for more.

He pulled his mouth from hers. Thrust her away.

The sound of their harsh breathing filled the small bedroom. The woman blinked up at him, confusion pulling her brows together. A flush rose along the delicate chords of her neck and across her collarbone. She'd been as affected by that kiss as much as he had. Satisfaction curled in his gut.

She ran her fingers along her lower lip, and he longed to trace that path with his tongue. Suck those fingers into his mouth. All the torment and hunger and wanting torturing his body when he awoke from his dreams with her was magnified tenfold, a hundredfold, for having the real thing in his arms. This wasn't a dream…was it?

"You're real?" he asked, his voice raw and harsh.

Her nod was slow in coming.

Then he knew. The woman in front of him wasn't some dream girl his imagination had conjured to taunt him in the night. The haze that seemed to surround her in his dreams was gone. She lay before him in sharp focus. Osborn remembered the utter helplessness he'd felt, raged against, when he tried to draw her back to him that last time. How he'd failed.

Somehow she'd put herself there. She was responsible for all the anguished desire he'd felt. All his want. Need. His yearning for something he could never have.

Thought he could never have.

His.

Yes, she was his.

His berserkergang was wrong to back down, assessing the woman in his bed posed no risk. Everything about her was a threat to him. And still the chill signaling the approach of his berserkergang did not hit him.

Something must have been in his eyes, or the set

of his lips must have alerted some self-preservation instinct inside her. He reached for her again.

And that's when she screamed.

Chapter 3

Breena had never been so terrified in her life. She's always thought that if she actually met up with her warrior in the flesh she'd be frightened… and she was right. The man who'd woken her up—his face tight with desire, outrage and stunned disbelief—was huge. Broad shouldered with the kind of muscular arms that easily proved he wielded a sword. Fearsome. A fighter.

Although he wasn't fighting, whatever was inside him drove him right at her. He quickly approached her, leaning toward her with determination and intent burning in his eyes.

What he intended to do, she didn't fully know, as her dreams never really went much further than the kissing, but whatever it was…it had to be dangerous.

There was a reason princesses were locked up in towers and hidden away in far-off places, guarded by magical creatures. It was to keep those princesses safe from the kind of danger this man radiated. Because despite her fright, some small part of her wanted to know what all that danger was about. She screamed louder.

His hand covered her mouth to stifle her.

That was the second time someone had muzzled her, and it would be the last. Maybe it was the food, or that she'd finally snatched a bit of rest or just plain fear, but Breena, princess of Elden, had had enough.

With every last bit of strength she possessed, she pushed at his shoulders, her scream changing to a grunt, then finally silent.

He didn't budge, but his hand fell away. The sound of her labored breathing filled the tiny space of the bedroom. His dark eyes searched her face, lingered at her breasts and followed down her legs. Then his gaze slammed into hers and he reached for her again.

"That's far enough," she said, scrambling to the floor, putting the bed between their bodies.

He lifted a brow at the protection she'd chosen. A bed—not the safest of barriers.

"Who are you?" she asked.

"I'll ask the questions," he told her, his voice gruff and rumbly.

Breena pursed her lips and nodded. The warrior did have a point, she *had* invaded his home.

"I've dreamed about you," he said, angry wonder lacing his words.

She'd been expecting questions, demands; instead, his statement sealed the connections she had with this man. Her dream lover. *Her* warrior.

She wet her bottom lip with her tongue. "You've been in my dreams, too," she admitted. *Because I put you there.* She'd just leave that little detail out of her explanations. Every instinct told her to be cautious, to not offer him too much information about herself.

"But there's never been fear in your eyes."

No, she could imagine what her gaze had conveyed in his dreams. A woman who wanted. Wanted *him*.

Faster than she thought such a large man could move, he was around the bed that separated them, and at her side. Crowding her. Breena took a step backward. And another. The wood-beamed wall of the cabin cut into her shoulder blades.

He'd backed her into the wall, and there was no escape.

"I've wondered a thousand times what your skin would feel like." The back of his hand smoothed down her cheek. His nearness was devastating to her senses. The scent of him, like the woods and fresh air, made her long to breathe him in deep. Heat radiated from his body, chasing away the chill to her skin from wearing tattered clothing.

Blood pounded through her body, rushed in her ears. Her eyelids fluttered at the first touch of his skin against hers. She'd been so alone for the past few days, so afraid, and his touch made her feel safe for the first time.

He'd wondered what she'd feel like outside of a dream. "So have I," she told him, and her fingers lifted to his face. Touched the line of his jaw.

His large hand captured her exploring fingers, drawing them to his lips. "Tell me your name." It was a gentle command. "I've wondered."

"Breena."

"Beautiful name," he said, his gaze lowering to her lips for a moment, then back to meet her eyes. "You look exactly as you appeared in my dreams." He dropped her hand to pull a twig from her hair, rub away some of the dirt from her cheek. "Who's done this to you?"

The caution she'd felt earlier returned. "The details are fuzzy."

Okay, not truly a falsehood. The fine points of how she'd arrived in this strange kingdom, how long she'd wandered around in the wilderness or even eaten, *were* fuzzy. She tried to concentrate, to come up with some piece of information that would allay his curiosity…but the only picture she could conjure in her mind was the sinister, bony frame. The frightening creature with the eight legs that made a shudder slide down her back. The blood of her parents spilled on the floor of the great hall where they'd once danced and once ruled over a kingdom. That was clear.

She swallowed down a quiet sob, her body quaking, remembering her terror that night.

"In my dreams there was no fear in your eyes. Don't be afraid of me." He reached for her hand again, drew her fingertips to his mouth. The warmth of his tongue sparked a carnal response from deep inside her. Breena found it hard to breathe, hard to concentrate on anything but this man. His warmth. His dark eyes, and what he was doing to her body with his lips.

Breena suspected he meant his actions to be soothing, or to draw her attention away from her fear. Instead, she was more afraid of him than ever.

The warrior drew her hand from his mouth and placed it on his shoulder. She sunk her fingers into the dark strands at the nape of his neck. She gasped when his lips grazed along her collarbone, his tongue teasing the sensitive place beneath her ear.

"Tell me why you're here," he urged.

To survive. To kill.

She shrugged her shoulders, wanting the voices

out of her head. Breena leaned her back against the wall, giving him better access to her body. Her skin. Her. "I don't know. I thought it was an accident that I found your cottage, but now…now I wonder if maybe I was drawn here."

He seemed to like her response because he tugged the lobe of her ear into his mouth.

Her throat tightened with relief. The man whose dreams she'd visited was perfect. She'd always dismissed her magic as being weak and inadequate, but her powers must have led her to the door that was the gateway into this man's dreams. A warrior who could help her return to Elden, defeat the invaders…just like those heroic princes from her stories.

"Now you can help me," she said, her body beginning to shiver as he traced the curve of her ear with his tongue. Even the feel of his breath, warm and heavy against her skin as he exhaled, did strange things to her body.

"Don't worry, I'll help you all you want." His voice was a promise.

"You can amass an army?" she asked, daring to run her hands along the broadness of his shoulders, delighting in the dozens of muscles roping his arms.

His lips stopped their exploration of her neck. "An army?" He leaned away from her, his eyes heavy-lidded and filled with desire and confusion. "Just what kind of help are you needing?"

"I only—"

But her warrior was already cutting her words off with a slicing arc of his hand. "My sword is not for sale." His gaze crept down to her breasts. "For any price."

"My family is in danger."

"It's not my concern," he told her, his voice indifferent, his stance nonchalant.

"But… You're supposed to…" she sputtered. He was her warrior. He was supposed to help her. Wasn't this some kind of requirement of the fairy-tale code?

His gaze dropped to her nipples poking at her shredded bodice. "I'll have Bernt try to find you some better clothes. But *you* are leaving."

For the first time since waking up in her bedchamber with Rolfe ushering her to safety, Breena felt completely worn out. Defeated.

Survive.

The command echoed through her head. That's what she was trying to do.

"I need your help."

He cupped Breena between her legs, and her breath lodged in her throat with a hiss. "If the help you need is here, I'm happy to please." His fingers caressed her sensitized skin, her tattered clothing hardly an obstacle. "And I *would* please you, Breena."

Her nipples hardened at the carnal guarantee in his words. Her skin heated, and she felt wetness between her thighs.

Then he dropped his hand. His expression grew hard. "That's all the help I'll be offering."

She watched as the man of her dreams left her to walk away, slamming the door behind her.

For months Osborn had woken up in an agony of frustration and wanting. Hunger and need for one woman. After holding the real thing in his arms, caressing her soft skin, tasting her sweet lips, he knew nothing could ever satisfy him.

Nothing but turning around, tossing Breena on her back and burying himself in her sweet flesh.

He couldn't remember when the dreams had first begun, and now he saw those dreams, those fantasies, for what they really were—nightmares.

His brothers were grouped by the kitchen table. The wood from the broken chair already swept away, the table clean of the leftover dried oatmeal. All traces of Breena's visit gone…except he felt her in his home now. Felt her presence in him.

His skin began to chill. His berserkergang grew wilder inside him. The walls of the cabin he'd built alongside his brothers, his sanctuary, now boxed him in and imprisoned him. "I have to get out of here," he told Bernt and Torben, grabbing his pelt bag and ignoring the curious glances of his brothers.

"What about her?" Bernt dared to ask.

Osborn turned on his brother, a roar of anger on his lips. "Get rid of her before I get back."

"But she's…" His younger brother Torben swallowed.

"What?" he bellowed his question.

"She's a girl."

And his cock knew it.

Bernt cleared his throat. "We thought maybe she could stay. Make our meals."

"And clean, and do the laundry. Girls like to do that stuff."

Obviously he'd kept his brothers away from civilization for too long. He could just add it to the list of his faults and deficits where his brothers' raising was concerned. "We're not a houseful of dwarves, and she's sure as hell not staying."

"But—"

Osborn shot his brother a look, and Bernt was smart enough to know when to shut his damn mouth.

"Get her some clothes and get her out of here." Osborn slammed the door behind him, making every beam of wood and pane of glass rattle.

"What do we do?" Torben asked.

Bernt shrugged. "Get her a pair of pants, one

you've outgrown. I'll see if I can find an old shirt and shoes small enough to fit her feet."

"I don't see why she can't stay," Torben said, happily defiant when his oldest brother wasn't around.

Bernt only shook his head. Nothing about today made much sense.

The door to the bedchamber opened, and the woman poked her head around the corner.

Breena had heard the voices from the other room. But then how could she not? She was pretty sure her warrior had left, and she was also plenty sure the hinges of the front door had taken a beating with his retreat.

Why was he so angry? It just didn't add up. Her magic had drawn her to him; it must have. Why would she be able to put herself into the dreams of a man so powerful, so fierce, one who could surely help her, help her family, if she weren't supposed to use that gift?

Two boys stared at her from the other side of the door. They had to be his brothers. They all shared the same dark hair and dark eyes. Tall and lean, like gangly youths, but soon they'd fill out and be as muscular as their older brother. The youngest might even grow to be taller than her warr—

Okay, she was tired of calling him *warrior.* "What's his name?" she asked.

The youngest looked over at his brother, as if

spilling that beast's name could be construed as some kind of betrayal.

"Osborn," the older one said. "And I'm Bernt and this is Torben. We're going to find you something to wear before you leave."

Osborn. She allowed his name to roll around in her mind. In all the nights she'd visited this man as he'd slept, she'd never really thought of him as something other than her lover. The warrior in her dreams. Never imagined him in real life, as a man with a family, and responsibilities and a name.

There was another personality trait many of the princesses shared in the stories she'd read, selfishness, and she'd only ever thought of Osborn as someone to help her.

But was hoping to protect her family selfish? Her kingdom and all her people were dying. In truth, they might even now be dead or enslaved.

Breena squared her shoulders. Osborn might want her far away from him, but she had no plans to go. Her magic had brought them together, and her warrior might be reluctant but he *was* going to help. She eyed the front door. Apparently he wanted his brothers to get rid of her before he returned.

Not going to happen.

Kings and princes might rule through sheer force of will and strength, but as her mother always told her, a queen knew how to get what she desired with nothing but a smile and her brain. And she'd taught those skills to her daughter.

Breena flashed that smile at the boys right now. "Thank you for your hospitality. I'm so sorry I broke your chair, and it was such a fine work of craftsmanship, too."

Bernt's cheeks began to flush. Flattery always worked on men.

Torben laughed. "You thought that chair was goo—"

The younger brother's words were cut off by a smack to his shoulder.

"I've been walking for so many days, and seen so many interesting things, but this cabin is…"

The brotherly irritation lining Bernt's forehead faded. "We haven't been outside our lands since—" he stopped, his brown eyes clouding "—well, for a long time. What's out there?"

Now this was very curious. She didn't know how long she'd roamed, but at least a couple of days, and she'd never once spotted another person. Osborn had apparently hidden himself and his brothers away from civilization for quite some time. Why?

Bernt looked more boy now than youth. She had him. A boy's sense of adventure was universal.

"It's a magical world out there."

Torben's eyes focused. "You've seen magic?"

She lowered her voice and leaned forward as if

she was about to impart a great secret. "I can do magic," she told him.

"Show me," he demanded.

Now she had him, too. She only had to draw out his curiosity until her missing magic reappeared.

She stretched her arms above her head. "Oh, I'd love to," she told them. Was she going overboard with the reluctance lacing her voice? "But it seems I have to be on my way." She aimed her steps in the direction of the door.

"Oh, but—"

"Maybe you can stay a little longer."

She flashed them a smile. "You did say something about clothes."

"And we have something that will take away the pain of your cuts and sunburn." The boys left her side in a sprint, Bernt rummaging through an old wooden chest by the window, while Torben vanished into the bedchamber. They both returned with well-worn but clean pants and shirts. About three sizes too big. But if for some reason she was back out wandering the woods again, the rugged material of her new outfit would protect her from the sun and the tree limbs.

"Tell us about what you've seen," Torben urged.

What would intrigue him besides her magic? Food always worked for her. "My favorite day is market day. All the tradespeople and farmers bring their wares and set up booths. Of course everyone gives you a little sample of their food so you'll buy. One walk down the aisle and you're completely full." Or so she'd been told by one of the maids who'd helped her dress. Her parents would never have allowed her to go to market day, so she had something in common with these two brothers who longed to experience something new and different.

"What kind of food?" Torben asked, licking his lips. "All we get here is porridge and meat. Burned meat."

"To a crisp," Bernt added. "Osborn is not a very good cook."

"And if we complain, he'd make us do it. Can you cook?"

She didn't exactly cook, but she knew how to direct a kitchen staff. "My favorite is stew." That wasn't a lie. She didn't specifically say she'd cooked it. "Thick with lots of vegetables and fresh baked bread."

Both boys closed their eyes and moaned.

"But there's more than just the booths. There's singing, traveling acrobats and minstrels and dancing bears."

Bernt's face grew angry. "Bears shouldn't dance."

She'd forgotten she was in Ursan lands. "It was only one time. I'd love to tell you more, but I better change clothes and start walking before it gets dark."

Torben slumped in disappointment. "I'd like to try that bread."

Breena began to finger the frayed edge of the pants they'd given her. "I'd hate to put on these fresh clothes when I'm so dirty. Is there somewhere I can take a bath?"

She'd only suggested a bath to stall time, but now that she'd said the request out loud, Breena actually longed to be clean. To wash the grass from her hair, the dried blood from her knees.

"We usually just hop in the lake."

"There's no bathing tub?"

The boys just looked at her blankly.

"I'm guessing you wouldn't have shampoo?"

Torben only nodded.

"Okay then, point me in the right direction."

Bernt's brow knotted. "I don't think this is a good idea."

"Technically I'll be out of the house, so he can't get mad," she assured him.

"Oh, he can get mad."

She just bet he could.

Osborn stalked through the woods, crashed though the tall grass and avoided the areas where the bears slept. Sweat slid down his back as he pushed himself to keep going. Away from his home and away from her.

He swiped at a branch closing in on his eye. Clearly he was going crazy. The isolation of his lonely life was making him want things he had no business wanting. What a fool he'd been. He'd clung to the woman who visited him as he slept. He hadn't realized how much until what he'd been fighting so hard to hold on to had been ripped away from him. At first he'd try to force his thoughts to something else during the day. Keeping the area around their cabin clear. Ensuring there was enough food and clean water. Taking care of his brothers. But finally he succumbed, and he'd work to remember those dream moments with her throughout his day. Although, truthfully, it wasn't very hard. Those moments drew him to his bed at night so he could dream.

But it wasn't special like he'd thought. He'd never imagined her to be real; otherwise, he would have dredged hell to find her. The elemental pleasure that tore through him the moment he'd realized his dream woman slept in his bed, lay in his arms, was alive for him, rivaled only by the primal satisfaction of joining the ranks of Ursan warriors.

Only the woman in his dreams just wanted him to kill for her. Like all the others who thought coin would keep them clean from the dirty work. Special? What in the hell had he turned into?

The heat and exhaustion finally took him over. Osborn stripped off his shirt to cool down, and his steps slowed. But the sun overhead beat down on him. He changed his course to the lake. How many times had he sought refuge from his thoughts, his responsibilities and the weight of the lives he'd taken in those chilly waters?

The splashing was what put him on guard. He sunk to his knees, reaching for the knife he always kept tucked in his boot. He quietly followed the trail of the intruder. They hadn't worked hard to cover their tracks. Or to be quiet. It sounded like…

He shook his head, but no… It actually sounded to him as if…

Osborn heard the beautiful sounds of a woman singing. His muscles tensed and his cock hardened. He cleared the brush blocking his view, the weapon in his hand forgotten. There, swimming in the blue water of his lake, was Breena. Naked.

Her ripped and worn clothes lay discarded in a heap by the bank. He spotted the pants and shirt loaned to her by his brothers neatly folded and waiting for her on a rock. The long blond strands of her hair floated around her shoulders, billowing in the water like something otherworldly and beautiful. He took a step, ready to touch it, touch her, before he stopped himself.

She'd had him under her spell for too long.

Breena let her feet land on the bottom, standing waist deep. With a smile, she reached toward the light filtering between the leaves of the trees that protected the lake he'd once thought idyllic. Now she'd invaded it, stamped her impression in this place that was once all his own. Sunlight glinted off the water drops rolling down her skin, and her wet hair plastered against her back, almost long enough to reach the most beautiful ass he'd ever seen.

This was how she was when he was alone with her in his dreams. She turned in the sunlight, beautiful and utterly delectable. Her nipples stood out between the wet strands of her hair, tempting him, drawing him closer. His for the taking.

Why was he the one walking away?

She was *his*.

He reached for the button of his pants, and they joined the clothes she'd tossed aside.

The water chilled his overheated skin as he chased her in the water. Breena turned toward him with a little gasp of surprise. Her cheeks were rosy from her exertion in the lake, her green eyes sparkling from the pleasure of her swim. He knew that pleasure. Now he would know another. In her arms.

She hadn't left his lands. Surely it would be easy enough to find another mercenary to kill whomever she wanted dead. There were plenty after his neck. But she'd stayed. She wanted him. Now he needed to know why. Needed to know almost as much as he needed to find the pleasure her sweet body offered. He grasped her chin, forcing her to look up at him.

"You put yourself in my dreams. Tell me the truth. You did it. You made me think of only you. Want only you."

Her nod was slow in coming.

He squeezed his eyes shut tight at her answer. Even now, some small sliver of hope, desire that she wanted him for more than a sword, still ached in his soul. Idiot. He sucked in a large breath of air. Then his gaze met hers. She pulled her chin from his grasp and shrank lower into the lake, the water sloshing over her lips. She looked more afraid of him than ever.

Good.

He always hunted best when his prey panicked.

Chapter 4

Breena bit back the urge to scream. What good would it do, anyway? From the looks of him, he'd only laugh. Osborn seemed to be pleased by her growing unease. As if he grew stronger from her fear.

Then she just wouldn't be afraid of him.

Ha! Impossible.

Her first, and really her only, instinct had been to shrink away from him, and shield herself with the water. And she wasn't exactly getting the reaction she wanted from him—to back away from her. Still, she wouldn't *show* her fear of him. She was a princess, and one of her singular skills was acting. "Why are you so angry with me?"

she asked, deliberately keeping her voice low and laced with the confusion she felt.

"You ask that?"

The man basically roared at her. A pair of birds took to the trees, and the leaves rattled. No one had ever dared to raise their voice to her. Not once in her entire life. Breena found she didn't much care for it.

"Your bellowing is scaring the wildlife."

His lips thinned, as if he were forcing himself to calm. "I don't bellow."

She almost destroyed their uneasy truce by lifting an eyebrow and replying with something verging on sarcasm. Her mother would be appalled at that kind of tone, but she'd learned it from her brother Nicolai. Her parents would be shocked at some of the stuff her brothers shared with a girl who was supposed to be a gently raised bridal prospect. Another wave of homesickness racked through her. Breena's throat tightened, but she quickly swallowed away the stiffness along with the sadness.

She needed this man's help. Desperately. Everything else she'd attempted to do to gain his attention had failed. Well, not everything. Her body had his full notice. Breena felt herself warm despite the coldness of the water. But he'd already proved she couldn't change his mind with kisses.

Neither did the logical approach of simply asking for his help.

But this was her warrior. There was no denying it. Why dream of him? Why did he dream of her, if he were not chosen for her?

Breena smiled sweetly. She'd get him to help her. Somehow and some way. "Of course you didn't bellow. My apologies." Even if she had to lie to make it happen.

His eyes narrowed. His gaze searched hers, obviously looking for signs of deception. Breena held her breath, willing every muscle of her face to remain slack. *I'm completely truthful.* His broad, tense shoulders began to relax.

Either he wasn't very good at spotting deception, or he scared everyone around him so much, no one dared to lie.

Or maybe he knew she was lying, and enjoyed the idea of making her think he believed her every word. She could go around and around with conjecture but what she needed was action.

"I never meant to upset you," she tried again.

The warrior made a scoffing sound. "You didn't upset me."

Yeah, he'd have to actually care in order to be upset. This hard man in front of her didn't appear as if he cared about much.

"Hurt?" she offered, enjoying going farther

down the path of "upset" when he clearly expected her to go the opposite direction.

He crossed his arms.

"Sad?"

His expression told her she was pushing it.

"Angry?"

"Closer."

"Enraged?"

"Closer still."

But his dark brown eyes no longer held a trace of ire. The tension never returned to those big shoulders of his, and his hands hadn't fisted at his sides. What do you know, the warrior in front of her had a sense of humor.

"Irritated?" she finally questioned.

"Irritated," he said with a nod.

Yes, she just bet he was. If she'd ever been allowed to bet.

"I apologize if I irritated you," she said formally.

Surprise flitted in his gaze until he promptly masked it.

Her mother wouldn't have been able to find fault with her apology. Except the part where she was naked. Wet. And standing in front of what she assumed was an equally naked man with only her hair as any kind of covering.

A princess at the Elden Court was seen but rarely heard.

"Your power comes with marriage," her mother

would often instruct Breena, "and the best marriages are arranged with a man who knows nothing about you. Can't know anything about you because you've been silent your whole life. Conduct yourself right, and there will be absolutely nothing any potential bridegroom can object to. Nothing his ambassadors can negotiate over on the marriage contract."

Even at the young age of eight, her mother's tutoring sounded bleak and lonely. Breena hadn't been very good at neutralizing her features then. The pout was already forming, the need to argue quick on her lips.

The memory played on. Queen Alvina squeezed her hand gently. "Once you command your own palace, your own kingdom, then you'll be the woman you were meant to be. Until then, observe. Watch the servers and the cooks and the seamstresses. Listen to their conversations, what concerns them. Learn to read the faces of the hunters and soldiers before they ever report to the king. Knowledge and understanding…that is how you rule." A girl could almost be forgotten when she lived among the shadows. Instincts alone told her when someone's words didn't match their expressions, as often happened with the visitors and foreign dignitaries who spoke with the queen and king in chambers.

Over time, she'd also grown to know the

feelings and emotions of her people with only a look or from a few hushed whispers. Such as when a kitchen maid was sad or one of the young huntsmen was in love. Her family might be vampires or wield powerful magic, but she could uncover what most people wanted to keep hidden. Like the proud man in front of her. Breena suspected this man held a lot of secrets. And she wanted to know all of them.

And wasn't she just bemoaning the dullness of her life not so long ago? Since then she'd been awakened, raced through her home in search of her brothers, been captured and brought before—

Something searing and painful lanced across her mind. Breena blinked back tears, either from the pain or from the memory, she couldn't be sure.

Avenge.

Survive.

The two conflicting commands battled inside her head, until she doubled over, gasping for breath.

"Are you all right?" He grasped her arm with his big hand a little too painfully. Perhaps her warrior was unused to touching females. A tiny thrill shot through her. The warmth of his fingers soothed and actually stopped the commands echoing in her mind.

She looked up at him. A sense of urgency filled her, and she suddenly grew desperate to make him understand. To *want* to help her. His touch could block the pain of her memories, could block the words echoing in her mind.

"What we talked about before…it's all true. My magic led me to you."

He made a scornful noise. His hand fell to his side, and the corner of his lip curled up in disgust. He didn't trust her. She sensed the man didn't trust many. What had made him, his life, so very hard?

But she'd seen him with his guard down.

In her dreams.

There he'd smiled. And laughed. And desired. And shared himself with her. The hard man in front of her now would hack off his own arm before baring his private thoughts, his soul, to anyone. Least of all to her. He probably viewed her as the woman forcing her way into his sleep, when he was most vulnerable. No wonder he didn't trust her and was so very angry with her. But she had to make him believe her.

It seemed her very sanity depended on it.

Breena reached for his hand again, needing the warmth of his touch, even if it wasn't freely given. "Please, you have to believe me. I didn't even realize you were real until I woke up…"

"Nearly naked in my bed." There was his growl again, but it didn't hold the kind of anger as before, but something was definitely pent up inside him. This was more to the man she'd opened her eyes to see earlier today. Much more to this warrior of her dreams. For some reason, that was even scarier.

She took a step backward.

"Good move."

She held her breath.

"But too late." He jerked her closer, and their bodies rubbed together.

Osborn lowered his head. The harsh line of his lips just an inch away from her mouth. Her gaze clashed with his. Fierce anger and hot desire burned in those brown eyes. An anger and desire she suspected simmered just below the surface of him.

"Use your magic on me now, Breena. Make me stop."

"I…I can't." She didn't want him to stop.

His mouth came down hard on hers, and her lips parted. His tongue pushed past her lips and found hers. Osborne's thick arms wrapped around her, and he drew her into the heat of his hard body. Her nipples pebbled against the hairy roughness of his muscled chest, and Breena's heartbeat kicked up to a runner's pace.

He smelled of chestnuts and the earthy scent of the deep woods. Her dreams never detailed how wonderfully he smelled. Or how he tasted of the sweetness of apples, and something unrecognizable to her she could only label it as man. *Him*.

Just when she was about to sink into heaven, Osborn took it away. His lips left, and he rested his forehead against hers. Panting. "Why can't you make me stop?" he asked, pulling away to see her face. His fingers grazed the back of her neck, and sweet sensation tingled along her damp skin.

"My magic…it's gone," she told him with a shrug.

Disappointment flashed across his eyes before it quickly faded. Or he masked it. *Come on, Breena, you're supposed to be good at reading people.*

He placed the barest of kisses against her mouth, and her bottom lip trembled. "Then *tell* me to stop, and I'll stop."

How could she when she ached to be in his arms? To draw his mouth down to hers? To finally *live* every emotion and sensation the Osborn of her dreams promised right now in real life.

She shook her head. "I can't."

His fingers began to caress the skin below her ears, never thinking how sensitive she was there. She watched as the muscles lining his throat worked. Something dark and slightly possessive flashed across his face, turning his features stony. But this wasn't scary. Oh, it was dangerous, and should be a warning, but it was so, so tantalizing.

He lowered his head, and this time she met his kiss, unafraid, and as an equal as when she lay on her bed and joined him in her dreams. The fear and the hunger and the pain of the past few days faded from her mind. Osborne took over. The delicious scent of him filled her. The harsh sounds of his ragged breathing pervaded her ears. The taste of him on her lips…

Breena wanted more.

Standing on tiptoe, she twined her arms around Osborne's neck, drawing him down as close as she could. She sunk her fingers into his long, damp strands of hair and she pressed her mouth to his with equal force.

Osborne groaned, the sound rumbling through his chest. His desire for her made Breena's stomach feel hollow, the way it did in her dreams. His hands began running up and down her back, and when she teased his tongue with hers, his hands finally stopped their quest and grabbed her backside, lifting and fitting her against the hard swell of his arousal.

Breena shivered as a wave of powerful desire sped through her. This incredible sensation was what the chambermaids giggled about at night when they didn't realize they could be overheard by their princess. What the young men of Elden fought battles over in the practice fields outside the castle walls. *This* is what drove her back to her dreams with him whenever she could. For the first time, Breena felt like she was living. Living what *she* wanted to live. Every sense, every pore, every part of her body, ached for more and more.

A harsh gust of wind blew through the trees, rustling the leaves and startling the birds. A shadow fell across the lake as dark clouds barred the sunlight. An eerie chill poured over her exposed skin, despite being wrapped in Osborn's arms.

He lifted his head, and she glanced toward the sky.

Something black and snakelike streaked over the treetops. Breena had never seen its like before, but her stomach tightened and grew queasy at the sight. "What is that…?" she began, but couldn't continue. Another formed in the sky, aiming toward them. She began to shudder, every part of her rejecting the horrifying entity charging for them. The vile thing oozed evil. It swallowed the sanctity of this soothing place, returning only fear and pain and a promise of misery.

Osborn swore, and glanced behind her back toward the pack he'd discarded on the bank. "My weapon," he whispered. "On my count, run toward it. But stay behind me."

They wouldn't make it. The bleak thought appeared in her mind out of nowhere. She shook her head, rejecting the hopelessness invading her soul. She knew the grim conviction in her mind had to be planted by the monsters in the sky.

"Now," he urged, still keeping his voice low so as not to alert the creatures coming for them. He jolted in front of her, spinning her around, and aimed for the bank. This water had once welcomed her, took away for a few moments all the pain she'd felt since she'd awoken in the strange land. Now that lake seemed to turn hostile. Heavy water swirled around her waist, tugging at her feet and dragging her down deeper into the depths.

"Resist," Osborn ordered over the harsh crashing of rushing water. "It senses your fear, but that thing has no power over you."

Breena propelled herself, pushing for each step she took. She had to be slowing Osborn down, preventing him from reaching his pack. "Keep going," she told him.

He shook his head, instead gripping her arm tighter, pulling her behind him. But it was too late. The tip of the entity began to wrap and wind itself around Osborn's free arm. His breath came out in a pained hiss, and she felt his body stiffen.

He dropped her arm and shoved her away from him. "Go, Breena. Get out of here and warn my brothers."

He turned and faced the creature, landing a blow with the kind of force that would have felled a large man. With one last burst of energy, she managed to drag herself onto the bank. The sound of the battle behind her was horrific. The creature shrieked as Osborn rained blow after blow along its snakelike skin, but still the beast never fully released him. His face grew red as he fought with nothing but his brute strength. Vines grew from the snake creature's sides. Osborn hacked at them with his bare hands.

With a hideous shriek, the creature struck Osborn across the side of his face. Blood seeped from a gash across his cheek, and began to bubble from the poison.

How could he fight? How could he win against something so vile? Burns marked where the creature had grazed his skin. Osborn sank to his knees. Struggled to stand.

Dark images flashed across her memory. A creature with razors for fingers. The sounds of the dying in her ears. The smell of death. Her head filled with pain. *No.*

All her muscles tensed and she began to shake. An angry energy began to build inside her. *No.* The word seemed to fill her ears, Blocking out any other noises.

Breena lifted her arms and pointed at the snakelike beast attacking Osborn. "No!" she shouted at the evil thing, and a hot bolt tore from her fingertips. The creature shrieked as if burned. Osborn fell to the ground as the beast turned and aimed straight for her. Fear knifed through her. She almost turned and ran.

But she was done with running away.

Breena locked her knees, faced the evil coming toward her and lifted her hands again.

That thing has no power over you.

If she could prevent the monster from hurting Osborn, she could do more. The thing sped toward her. Another bolt flew into the creature's side and it twisted with a shrill howl. She sent another and another, until sweat filmed her forehead and it grew hard to breathe. Then she sent one more.

With a final shriek, the creature broke apart in a burst of blood. Red gore fell to the churning water, as if the purity of the lake wanted to repel the carnage rather than absorb it. She expected the other creature in the sky to attack next. It circled twice above their heads, then slithered away into the horizon. Finally the water in the lake settled. The wind died down and the sky lightened.

Breena sunk to the ground. Her muscles shook as she struggled to breathe. Whatever energy she'd used to kill the creature sapped her of any strength. She looked around for Osborn. She spotted him still lying where the creature had dropped him. Beaten. Poisoned. Burned. And still he fought to help her get away.

Now he didn't move.

She choked back a sob. Her stomach tightened, and a fluttery panic filled her chest. "Osborn!" she shouted as she crashed through the shallow pools of water and sand, where he lay facedown. "Please be alive. Please." Breena didn't think she could take another death. Certainly not that of her warrior.

With a strength she managed to scrounge up from somewhere, she rolled him over. She gasped when she saw his face crossed by scratches and deep wounds. She smoothed the blood away with her wet hands, fear making her fingers shake.

"Osborn."

Nothing.

Breena leaned closer, getting her nose almost to his. "Osborn!" she yelled.

His eyelids snapped open. "If that's your idea of healing skills, you've got a lot to learn." He groaned.

Her shoulders sagged in relief, her damp hair falling and shrouding them from the sun.

"Thank you," she said.

"For what?" he asked, his breath fanning her cheek.

"I slowed you down." *And nearly got you killed.*

"I wouldn't have made it, anyway."

A realist. She liked that. Sort of. It would certainly take some getting used to. Breena was used to life in the castle where she rarely saw the struggles of others. Was protected from it. Osborn would never lie to her. *That's* what she needed.

"Those things were too fast." His words were

grim. His eyes narrowed and his expression turned stony again. Whatever fog he'd been in since she'd rolled him over was dissipating. Her angry warrior was back.

He pushed himself up.

"You shouldn't be trying to sit yet. I think you need to rest."

He only glared at her, and flexed his arms, then his legs, checking for injuries. He hissed in a breath. He'd obviously found one.

She reached for him. Breena had only meant to pat his shoulder, offering a touch of compassion. But her intended comforting brush of her palm turned into a near caress. She'd never been so close to a man before, especially not one who was naked and so, so fascinating. At least, not while she was awake. She still had the taste of him in her mouth.

Every tendon and sinew of his body was tight and defined. Powerful muscles roped his chest, and bunched at his arms. Scars—some old, some new—ran along his body. And he'd have new ones today. "I'm sorry," she told him again, already leaning forward, her lips just inches away from his skin.

His fingers circled around her hand, drawing her touch away from his warm skin. "What have you done?"

The anger lacing his every word broke her from her daze.

"Done?" Breena began to shake her head. "I haven't done anything."

Yes, her angry warrior was definitely back, this time tinged with a streak of suspicion.

In one quick movement, his hands were at her hips. He rolled her over, her back pressing into the damp sandy bank. He straddled her, blocking any opportunity for her to get away.

"What have you brought here? To my home?" he bellowed at her, his finger digging painfully into her shoulders.

"I don't know."

He leaned in, their noses almost touching. "Those creatures…those *things,* that was magic. Blood magic."

Her heart began to pound, and her throat grew dry. *Blood magic.*

The idea of it repelled her. Every part of her—every emotion, every thought, every memory—rejected it and was sickened by the words.

Blood magic could only work by taking of the blood of the unwilling. Forced. Drained until dead.

"You know of these?" she asked. Dreading his answer, hoping it was something he battled on a regular basis here in Ursa and not something she'd brought down on their heads. But a memory, a flash of recognition of the magic, nagged at her. Then the pain returned.

"In places, but not here. *Never* here."

His confirmation made her shake. She'd brought the magic of death to this peaceful place. For a moment her thoughts lingered on the poor soul whose blood had created such a thing. How they'd experience excruciating pain, and then praying, even begging, for death. A death denied.

"Those things travel in pairs, so one can always lead more here. To my home."

With his weight pinning her to the ground, Osborn moved his hands from her shoulders. She began to shake as his fingers traveled over her naked skin, traced the line of her collarbone until meeting at her neck.

"When I came here I made a vow to kill anything that threatened Ursa ever again. Endangered what was left of my family."

His thumbs caressed the soft skin of her throat. One press, that would be all that it would take, just a little force from his thumbs, and he'd deny her breath. His gaze slammed into hers. "Tell me, Breena. Tell me why I shouldn't kill you."

Chapter 5

He'd never killed a woman.

It was his rule when he hired out his sword to anyone who had the coin. His only rule. An Ursan warrior never fought until forced and only to protect his family and his homeland. What he'd done to survive, to ensure his brothers' survival, would have brought shame to his people. In those early days after leaving Ursa, he'd sunk to the lowest depths. He lived with other mercenaries, men who'd kill him in his sleep to get his job, or just for the pleasure of watching him bleed.

He'd worked for the grasping, greedy overlords who cared more about securing their own power than taking care of their people. They starved while his people, whose rulers were just and fair, died. But those thoughts always led to madness. Hell, he had been a little crazy after he fled his homeland with his brothers. The harsh, pained sounds of the dying people echoed in his ears. The echoes only silenced when replaced by the cries of his young brothers begging for a mother who wouldn't come to comfort them. Would never come.

Only cheap ale and a few moments' pleasure in a paid woman's bed drowned out the noise. A part of it.

Then he'd broken his own rule. He was paid to kill a young girl, no more than ten. All for the sake of more power. More coin. The girl's only crime was her marriage alliance. She was promised to a boy who'd one day be king of his lands. A rival family had a daughter of their own they wanted to see sitting upon the throne.

He located his intended victim sleeping in her bed. Her tiny hand curled around a doll. He'd found his own sister this way many times.

What had he become? The blood of honorable warriors flowed through his veins. He was one with the bear…and he was about to cowardly cut the neck of a small girl. He'd stuck his dagger into the wooden chest next to her bed as a warning to her family, grabbed his brothers and fled into the night.

He prayed to the spirits of the bears that they might let his family enter their sacred grounds, and he vowed to protect those lands with his life, even to kill any trespasser who dared to enter the domain of the bear.

And here she was. The person who dared to defy the warnings staked on the outskirts of this isolated land and intrude where she had no right to be.

Osborn looked down at the woman stretched naked beneath him. Her very presence mocked his vow and his rule—to never kill a woman—and yet he must kill. She brought menace, blood magic, the worst kind, here.

Her breasts rose and fell as she took one ragged breath after another. The tight dusky tips invited his touch and his tongue and he was distracted for a moment. Her hair splayed all around the ground, like it did when he dreamed of her. She wore only an odd timepiece around her neck. Her soft lips were parted and a pulse hammered at the base of her throat.

He was distracted longer than a moment because she slammed her knee into his side. His breath came out in a grunt, but he didn't budge. It would take more than a small woman's shove to overpower him. He gripped her wrists and tugged them high above her head to prove his point.

"Are you daring me to kill you, Breena?"

"Let me go!" She bucked her hips, trying to shake him off, but only managed to shift her legs so that she cradled him. He felt the slick heat of her woman's body, and his cock stiffened. How long had it been since he'd touched a woman? Since bringing his brothers here, he'd driven every emotion, pounded every desire and drove every wish he'd once had for himself into creating something on this land. Raising his brothers, keeping them alive, making sure they had a life so that when he left to seek revenge on those who'd brought down the destruction of his family, his brothers could and would carry on without him.

In an attempt to dislodge him, Breena jerked against his cock, and his breath came out in a hiss. Years. It had been years since he'd sunk himself into a woman's inviting warmth. But the female beneath him wasn't just any female; she was the woman of his dreams.

No. She was the woman who'd invaded his dreams and made him dream of her.

"You cannot best me."

"I can try," she told him, meeting his gaze. Defiance and something like desperation mingled in the green depths.

He knew those sentiments.

Felt them.

Lived them.

She shouldn't have to feel that.

Why he should even care, he couldn't fathom. But for some reason, Osborn cared. It had been a long time since he'd really given a damn about anything.

Her bottom lip trembled for a moment, and he couldn't look away from the tempting softness of her mouth. Then he felt her spine stiffen. "If you're going to kill me, do it now, otherwise—"

Her "otherwise" was punctuated with the top of her head meeting his chin. His teeth snapped together, and his head reared back, but the shock of her action didn't loosen his grip. Instead, he shifted both her wrists to just one of his hands and gripped her chin to make her meet his eyes. Just to prove that he could.

"A moment ago I was thinking I wouldn't kill you. I'm back to thinking I will."

"I…" But her sentence trailed. Had he expected her to apologize for wanting to live?

Her one word drew his glance back to her lips. The tempting seductress of his dreams, or the sleepy enchantress come to life. Now Breena was a woman. Naked. And under him.

Osborn lowered his head, and took from her what he'd wanted. And she gave it to him. Her lips met his, her mouth opening to welcome in his tongue.

She tasted like promise and better than his dream.

He wanted to taste all of her

"Please," she said, her voice broken and needy.

Please what? Please don't kill her? Please make her feel something other than fear for a moment? Fear he'd caused?

He slumped against her, burying his face in her drying hair. The drive to explore her body died, and was replaced with something less primal. Guilt? Regret?

He didn't need more of that in his life. He had enough for a dozen lifetimes.

"I won't kill you."

He felt her sag beneath him, the fight draining from her limbs. He released her hands, and balanced above her, Breena's sweet, soft curves still cradling him. "But I need answers." He eyed the sky, noting the position of the sun. "It will be dark soon. You can stay tonight, but you leave tomorrow after I'm satisfied I know all I need to about this threat. And, Breena…"

"Yes?"

"Don't come back."

She nodded, and a smile almost tugged at his lips at the quickness of her agreement. "Don't worry."

With one more hard glare, he gently pushed himself off and away from her.

Don't look.

With a new determination, he began to examine

the wounds on his arm. Already a dark bruise had formed, mimicking the shape of the creature's snakelike body. The bleeding had stopped, though. The poison's ache had been reduced to a throb, and the burns would fade. He'd had worse. Osborn heard her rolling to her knees.

Don't look.

He felt the gash on his forehead, and wasn't surprised when he pulled back his hand to find it red with blood. That bang to the head might require his brother to take a needle to it.

Leaves crunched beneath Breena's feet as she raced quickly toward her clothes.

Don't look.

He looked. And groaned. Breena's slight frame was perfection. Made for a man's touch. *His* touch. Her backside was made to cup a man as he entered her from behind. His favorite position. His cock stiffened again.

"One more thing."

She turned, shielding her body from his eyes with her clothes. But she'd never be able to block the image of her soft curves from his memory.

"Until you go in the morning…don't let yourself be alone with me."

Breena dressed as quickly as she could with shaking fingers. Shaking everything. Even her knees felt weak. Her nipples ached when she pulled the shirt Osborn's brothers had loaned her over her head. The fabric felt rough and abrasive against her sensitized skin. Sensitized from his hands.

Don't let yourself be alone with me.

She closed her eyes and steeled herself against the hot wave of desire that coursed through her. The pleasure and the thirst for his touch narrowed her focus to only him. Her warrior. Osborn.

She licked her lips, finding them swollen. Breena lifted her fingers to touch where he'd touched. To trace along her bottom lip the spot he'd nipped.

Don't let yourself be alone with me.

A powerful warning. An order. And Breena had been raised to be an obedient girl. She'd never broken a rule or voiced a disagreement. Looking over her shoulder, she stole a glance at that man who'd issued what basically amounted to a threat—to her body. She began to shiver.

Osborn stood watching her. More like stood guard. His arms were crossed against his chest, the muscles coiled and ready for combat. His wide-legged stance instantly instilled caution to any observer.

I'll chase.

Run you down.

Render you defenseless.

He didn't care that he still stood naked. A flutter tickled her stomach. She'd never seen what made a man a man before, and she couldn't help but look. That part of him stood out and seemed to rise higher and bigger under her inspection.

Her imagination played with the idea of taking off at a run. He'd chase. He'd catch her. She'd be helpless against his strength. And while he'd threatened her with death a moment ago, she knew that was the last thing he wanted to do to her. He *did* want to do things to her. Forbidden deeds. She shivered again. Her skills were few, but along with hairbrushing there was the reading of people.

And she could read this man.

Probably the only weapon she had against him.

He was angry. He saw himself as betrayed by her and by his very dreams when he was at his most vulnerable. To a man like her warrior, such a thing was probably unforgivable.

She had to make him forgive her. It was the only way to get his help. Breena desperately needed his help, but, even more, she wanted him to *choose* to help her now that she'd kissed him. Been held in his arms. She craved that almost as much as she needed his skills as a fighter.

Breena had longed for this man. Ached for him. And now he stood just feet away from her…despising her. And wanting her with a heat that made her stomach dip in excitement.

Osborn's expression grew fiercer. His face was

as hard as the stone that made the walls of her bed-chamber at home.

Her fingers stilled. A new image…a memory of her home. And it came without pain. A rush of images and feelings nearly overwhelmed her. A peaceful kind of hope settled in her chest, and she smiled, barely realizing she was still staring at Osborn.

His hands fisted, and the muscles of his legs bunched as though he was about to stalk over to her and help her dress. Or remove what she'd already donned. Her mouth went dry, and she turned away, quickly returning to her task.

The thoughts of her home gave her peace, but menace tinged the calmness and the longing. She tried to concentrate, grab the memories, which seemed to be fluttering just out of her reach. This time the pain splintered behind her eyes, and she stopped trying to recall the elusive thoughts of home. But she'd try again. She'd managed to survive another day. She'd found her warrior, and soon she'd understand why she was so far away from her family.

She tugged on the rest of the clothes Bernt and Torben had given her, although *tugged* wasn't really the right word, since the garments still hung down past her fingertips, and she had to roll the pant legs up several times. Osborn was dressed in half the time it took her, and for that she was grateful. How was a girl, long shielded from males, supposed to react when encountering a naked man? And one so beautifully made? She still had to suffer staring at the broadness of his back, and how the pants clung to his seat. Was a woman supposed to find a man's backside attractive? She'd heard the maids in the castle gossip about a man's flat stomach, speculate on the largeness of his feet, or discuss the strength of his arms, but never specifically his—

"Hurry."

Startled, Breena met Osborn's gaze. *Caught.*

"We have a good ten-minute walk back to the cottage, and the sun will be setting soon. I want to be prepared if those things come back."

She nodded, and quickened her pace. Maybe he hadn't noticed her gawking at his body.

"And, Breena…"

"Yes?"

"You can look at that later. All you want."

Why did that sound less like a threat and more like something she'd want to do?

The brothers stood outside the cottage examining the waning daylight as they approached. Osborn had led the way, with her following close behind. The boys looked a little shocked to see her beside Osborn. Curiosity radiated from their young faces, and they loped down the stairs to meet them in the clearing.

"Did you see that thing in the sky?"

"It got all dark."

"What happened to your arm?"

Both boys spoke at once, and she smiled. Her brothers when they were younger also charged all over each other's words.

Her breath came out in a gasp, but the three males didn't seem to notice. Another memory without pain. Were her brothers safe? Where were they? Dayn had been outside, and Micah… She tried to picture his sweet face and remember. Something about his nanny. A shaft of pain forced her to stop digging for the memory of that night. It seemed she could recall the events much easier when she wasn't even trying. Perhaps she shouldn't try to force anything. Maybe she could ease into her past like she did her dreamhaze. Relax, picture a door in her mind and, instead of a dream, walk into her past.

"*We* were attacked."

Torben and Bernt didn't miss the emphasis Osborn placed on the word *we.* Subtlety was apparently not one of his skills. The brothers glanced at each other, and suspected they would have rolled their eyes if Osborn hadn't been standing right there.

"We sent them away."

"Just like you said," Bernt defended.

"I found her splashing around in the lake. That's where we were attacked."

"What were those things?" Torben asked.

"Scouts. Created by blood magic. I've seen them before, but only once."

"I've never seen anything by blood magic," Torben said, excitement lacing his voice.

A little too much excitement. Osborn glared down at his younger brother. "Pray that you never do."

"There's rumors you can hear the cries of the souls of whose blood was taken," Bernt added, clearly not wanting to be left out of the conversation.

Osborn's face turned grim. "It's a sound I have no wish to hear again."

"Their shrieks were horrible," Breena added, and she couldn't repress the shudder. She didn't know if the wailing came of the soulless or not, but she recognized misery, unbearable pain. So evil…

"That's because you are a girl," Torben replied. He turned his attention back to Osborn. "I guess they didn't shriek for long after you were done with them."

Breena bit back a smile at the pride the youngest brother felt over Osborn's prowess and fighting skill. Micah had been the same about Dayn and Nicolai.

Another thought of home without pain. Yes, the key was to let it flow naturally, and not work too hard.

Osborn cut a quick glance in her direction, then focused once more on his brothers. "I, uh, didn't have my pack."

"But, Osborn, you're never without your pack," Torben said. The boy sounded incredulous.

"You always keep it within reach."

Did she see a hint of color along Osborn's cheekbones? He cleared his throat and crossed his arms against his chest. What kind of move was that? It was as if he were trying to shield himself. Finally the man didn't have the upper hand.

"Yes, Osborn, why did you have your pack so far away?" she asked sweetly.

His brown gaze narrowed. "Turns out I didn't need it," he said between clenched teeth.

She met his stare. "Oh?"

Osborn shrugged. "Breena killed the beast."

Breena stood a little straighter. Yes. Yes, she had killed the thing. Of course, she had the help of a little magic.

The two boys stared at her for a moment. Then Bernt began to laugh. His younger brother quickly followed. Breena might be wearing borrowed clothes, not have much memory, but she knew one thing...she didn't much care for being laughed at.

The energy she'd felt at the lake began to swirl within her.

"Ouch," Torben said as he backed up a step.

Bernt stopped laughing long enough to look at his brother. "What—ouch!"

"It's like someone pinched me right on the as—er, backside," Torben said.

Osborn cut a quick glance her way, but he didn't look angry at her use of magical powers.

"What was that?" Bernt asked as he rubbed his rear.

"Looks like you just got a taste of what those blood magic scouts received."

Both boys glanced her way, their faces going from incredulous to betrayed. Then both boys slammed their attention back to their older brother.

"But you said girls were good for one thing. And that wasn't magic or fighting."

Now it was her turn to turn her attention to the big man at her side. "And what one thing is that?" she asked, almost afraid to know.

Osborn's expression turned blank. "Cooking."

"Cleaning," the boys said at the same time.

Osborn shrugged. "I guess there were two things."

She shot him a look full of venom. She'd never even glanced at another person in a cross manner in her life. Half a day in this family's presence and she was shooting energy daggers. At least he didn't suggest to these two boys that girls were only good for what happened once the chamber door was closed. Especially since her body was the only thing Osborn had showed much interest in when it came to her.

"You can't take help from a girl," Bernt said. "A warrior defeats alone."

Osborn dropped the pack at his feet and draped an arm over the shoulders of his brothers. He bent his knees so he'd be on eye level with them.

"There's no shame in a man accepting help from another warrior, even if she's a girl."

All this talk was beginning to fray on her nerves. Her father would be lost without his wife. The queen and her husband always stood side by side. He listened to her counsel, and shared the responsibility of ruling. At least Osborn seemed to have an inkling of how it was supposed to work. Unfortunately, he hadn't shared that with the two boys he was responsible for until apparently this moment. Her magic began swirling again, but she quickly tamped it down.

"Let's get inside. I'm hungry, and Breena has a lot of questions to answer. Bed after supper. I'm taking Breena into the village at first light."

"To the village? Can I go?" Bernt asked.

"It's been so long since you've taken us to a town."

Osborn shook his head. "Not until I know the threat."

The two boys slumped, then lumbered up the stairs. She was hungry again, too. Strange how the body had a timetable all its own. Her family was lost, she'd wandered around in a wilderness, been attacked, and yet, she could eat like it was any normal day.

"Why do your brothers think so little of girls?" she asked when they were alone.

His gaze lowered to her lips. Then fell to her breasts, and her nipples tightened and poked at the material of her shirt. "If you tell yourself a woman is good for only one thing, then you don't miss all the other things you desire from her."

His voice was filled with yearning, and so much loneliness she lifted her hand to cup his cheek.

His fingers grasped hers. His palm was callused, his grip tight, reinforcing her earlier musings that he hadn't spent a lot of time with females.

"Remember what I said? About not being alone with me?" he asked, his expression fierce.

She nodded, unable to take her eyes off his lips.

Osborn lowered his head, his mouth just an inch from her ear. "You're alone with me."

A warning, a threat, a promise… His words were all three. A shiver slid down her back. She squeezed her eyes shut tight as the soft touch of his tongue traced the curve of her neck.

"Breena?"

She nodded, wishing for more of this kind of caress. Wishing he wouldn't send her away in the morning. Wishing for so many things lost.

"Get inside."

Breena slipped out of his unresisting arms, and shut the door firmly behind her. She slumped against the rough wooden door, dragging in air and willing her heartbeat to slow down.

Survive.

Revenge.

She'd do both with Osborne's aid. Her dream magic was not wrong. Now all she had to do was get him to see it, too.

"Did you see that?" Torben whispered. "She touched him, and he didn't even yell. Or push her."

Bernt nodded. "I don't think things are ever going to be the same again."

Chapter 6

Dinner was a simple meal of tough bread, dried meat and berries she suspected were picked near the cabin. It was also completely silent. At Elden, dinner was a grand affair, with numerous courses, entertainment and lots and lots of laughter. Here, the three males regarded their food seriously, heads over their plates, and eyes steady on their meals.

"Does anyone know a funny tale?"

Bernt looked at her as if she'd suddenly begun speaking in another language. Her father always told such funny stories about his travels as a youth. Her mother could charm anyone with her tales of legend and myth. Nicolai told a great joke about a traveling king, a chastity belt and a trusted knight complaining about the wrong key.

Her gaze darted to Osborn and she felt her cheeks heat. She'd always thought that the funny part of that joke was that the king handed over a key that didn't fit. Now she realized it was the knight trying to remove the chastity belt and that the king had purposefully given the wrong key—that was what made the tale funny.

Breena would smack her brother when she saw him. She'd told that joke at least three times. A pang of homesickness chased away her anger. No, if she ever saw Nicolai again, she'd hug him.

"Do *you* know a funny story?" Bernt asked.

She was alive, she was safe for the moment and her belly was finally getting full. One meal. Breena could snatch one meal, and not worry about her brothers, her home or how she was going to survive tomorrow. Pushing the plate aside, she lowered her voice to that same conspiratorial tone her mother's took when she was about relay something interesting.

"Well, did you hear about the king of Alasia who was most displeased with his fortune-teller?"

Both boys leaned forward. "No."

"He told the king his favorite horse would die. And sure enough, the animal fell dead two days later."

"Fortune-tellers aren't real," Torben said, his

voice turning skeptical. She could only imagine where he'd acquired that attitude.

But Breena only gave what she hoped amounted to a mysterious shake of her head. "The king didn't trust him, either. In fact, he suspected the fortune-teller poisoned the horse so that his prediction would come true. That way, people from all over the kingdom would know of his skills, and give him money to relay their fortunes."

"What happened next?" Bernt asked.

"The king confronted the fortune-teller and dared him to reveal the date of his own death."

Bernt was practically squirming in his chair. Had no one told these boys stories? "Why?"

"Because the king was going to kill him," Osborn said.

Breena smiled over at the clever warrior. "Your brother is right. The king would kill the fortune-teller so that any answer he gave would be wrong, and no one would remember him."

Torben was off his chair raising an imaginary sword. "So what did he do? Run or challenge him to battle?"

She bit her bottom lip. No wonder her mother had so much fun telling stories around the table. "He did neither."

"What?" both boys asked.

"He looked the king in the eye, and said, 'I don't know the exact day of my death, but I do know that the king will follow me to the grave just two days later.'"

Osborn began to laugh, the sound of it delightfully rusty. She glanced his way and their gazes met. The desire in his gaze made her smile fade. Oh, she knew he wanted her body, but some other need for her lingered in his brown eyes. Her lips parted, and some elemental part of her wished to give him what he hungered for.

"Time for bed," he told his brothers without breaking his stare.

"What?"

"It's still early."

Osborn sighed heavily. "You'll need your rest if I decide you can go into the village. *If.*"

The brothers scrambled to clear the table and head into the room where she'd found the three beds earlier, and in just a few moments, she was alone with him. Again.

"Join me by the fire," he said. It wasn't much of a request, and when he offered her his hand, there was no way it could be disguised as courtly manners. She *was* going to sit next to him by the fire and she *would* be telling him everything he wanted to know.

Every great hall held a large fireplace, and even though the cottage was small, Osborn's hearth seemed to dominate one entire wall. An inviting, fluffy rug lay before the large, flat stones in front of the firebox. She sank down on the throw, seeking its softness. It was thick enough to be a sleeping pallet. Osborn's brothers had added extra blankets. At home, most people slept before the fire, warmed their hands near the flames and danced in front of it during celebrations and heated their ale over it. Osborn seemed to prefer to stare into it. Glare.

"You'll be leaving here at first light."

Was he telling her or himself? He'd already announced he'd be taking her to the village in the morning. It was all decided. Wasn't it?

"Already things are changing, and you've only been here a few hours. My brothers are unused to the gentleness a woman brings into a home. They're wanting things. Things that are impossible." His expression grew grimmer as he continued to peer into the flames. "You have to go."

Yes, yes. He'd already said that.

"No matter how many times you ask to stay."

Breena hadn't asked. Her heartbeat quickened, and she felt a little tingle all the way down to her toes. She was doing a pretty poor job of reading the strong man in front of her. She couldn't fathom his thoughts. No, she'd missed understanding his thoughts again.

Breena left the warmth of the rug and stood beside him. His height dwarfed her. The broadness of his shoulders filled her vision. She placed her hand in the middle of his back, and felt his muscles contract under her fingertips.

"Are you wanting me to ask, Osborn?"

He turned then, catching her off guard and imprisoning her hand between his. "I need to know what dangers you have brought here. Tell me how you got here."

The solid strength of his hand was exactly what she yearned for after wandering around hungry and tired and full of fear. "I don't really know. It's the truth." Half-truth. Why did she still feel the need to keep all of what she knew to herself? *Survive.* Some instinct told her to tell Osborn only what he needed to know so he'd help her.

"Then tell me what you do know."

"My home was attacked, the details are fuzzy. I woke up in this strange land."

"So you didn't see the markers telling you to keep out?" he asked, his voice filled with hostility and disbelief. His eyes scanned her face, searching for truth.

"I saw the bear skulls, so I figured I was on Ursa land, but they all died out. Years ago. So I assumed I was alone."

"Not all," he said, taking his gaze from her face and returning it to the fire.

Now Osborn's suspicious nature and overprotectiveness of his brothers made sense. They were the last of their kind. The last of the Ursans. Would she be the last of her people? Was she? A tragic trait to have in common.

But at least she had hope. Hope that her brothers and some the people of Elden had escaped. Osborn had none. "I'm sorry" seemed so insignificant to say about his loss, but she told him, anyway.

His throat tightened. "You're the first person to tell me that."

Sensing that was all the acknowledgment Osborn wanted to give to the tragedy that took his family, she went on with her story. "My people are magical. Not blood magic. Never. But my mother's powers are very strong. I believe she cast me from our kingdom."

"Why here?"

"Maybe something inside me chose the location. We'd been connecting through our dreams...."

His gaze burned for her as hot as the fire warming her cheek. Then his eyes narrowed. "You said you lost your powers, but you defeated the blood magic scout."

"You remembered that." Since he hadn't mentioned it, she thought he'd forgotten she'd told him her magic no longer worked.

"Another one of your lies?"

She shook her head. "When I woke up here, there were just two thoughts in my mind. To survive and to kill. Avenge. My magic was gone and whenever I try to concentrate and really remember what happened in my home…all I get is pain. It's like something is stabbing me behind the eyes, it hurts so bad. Believe me, if I could have used my powers when I was wondering around in that forest with no shoes and nothing to eat, I would have."

The corner of Osborn's lip turned up in a half smile.

"When your home was attacked, did you hear the cries we heard today? Creatures of blood magic?"

Breena closed her eyes, and tried to remember what she could before the pain hit her. All around her had been confused commotion. The sounds of battle and the wails of the wounded and dying. A flash of something sinister. A creature with razors for hands. A thing more skeletal than man. She sagged to the floor, and drew her knees up close to her chest.

"Yes, it was blood magic."

Osborn's breath came out in a heavy growl.

She looked up at him quickly, his face as harsh as it had been at the lake. "I'm so sorry. I never meant to bring danger to you or to your brothers."

He swallowed, closed and opened his fists a few times, then he nodded. "I know you didn't. Tomorrow I take you to the village. The scouts will be coming after you again. I don't want you leading them here."

"You really won't help me?" she asked, more

for her benefit rather than needing confirmation from him. She needed to say the words, so she could know she was truly alone. So her heart could accept the truth, and even the tiniest of hope she still held within her would die.

His silence was her answer.

"I'm sorry I brought all this down over your head. You are not the man I should be dream sharing with. I guess my magic got it wrong," she told him with a shrug. "I really thought you were the one for me."

Osborn pushed himself away from the hearth with a hard shove. She was surprised the cottage wall didn't give way. "I'll find you a pillow," he said, and stalked toward the chest in the corner where they kept the extra winter bedding.

His brother was on him the moment he entered the room. "She should sleep in here," Bernt told him, his glance roaming to the door. "It doesn't feel right. She's a girl. She shouldn't have to sleep on the cold floor."

Osborn sighed at his brother's misplaced gallantry. "You set out enough blankets to rival a mattress. She'll be comfortable enough in front of the fire. Besides, you willing to give up your bed?"

Bernt squared his shoulder. "Yes."

"*I'm* not."

"I just said I'd sleep out there."

Osborn shook his head. "And her sleep in here

with two males? That's even worse." He tossed his shirt at the foot of the bed and made a show of stretching his length along his mattress. "Either the three of us sleep out there or the three of us sleep in the comfort of our own beds. You know what I'll choose."

Bernt's breath came out in a huff. His little brother knew when he'd been beat. And he didn't like it. He slowly peeled his shirt up and over his head and then slid beneath the pelts covering his bed. Osborn blew out the candle, and darkness surrounded them. He felt his brother's uneasiness. It would keep the boy awake all night.

"You worried about her being a girl, think what sleeping in the house with us unchaperoned will do to her. Far worse than sleeping on a pile of blankets in front of a warm fire. The sooner she's out of here the better."

Soon the even breathing of his brother's sleep filled the room, but Osborn couldn't force his muscles to relax. If anything he grew more tense.

I really thought you were the one for me.

Her words were like a deep cut.

When he dreamed with Breena, he was someone else. When she admitted she put herself into his dreams he wrestled with temptation. He wanted to be the man in the dream for her.

But in his dreams, his blood never covered her hands. She'd brought this danger, but he brought much more. His dream girl didn't belong with him. But for the first time, Osborn wished he could mean something to someone.

What he'd told his brothers was the truth. The sooner Breena was gone, the better it would be. For all of them.

Breena awoke in the morning in front of the dying fire. Dawn crept over the line of the trees, and she heard a few birds begin their morning song. So normal. So idyllic.

She glanced down at her hands. They looked the same as they always did. Same nails. Still the same little freckle on the back of her hand. Her pinky finger stretched just a tiny bit crooked at the end.

But with her hands she wielded powerful magic. She pointed in the corner. Nothing. With her hands she wielded powerful magic *sometimes*.

Why did her magic power suddenly appear—now? Why not days ago when she could have put the power to use helping her family? What had changed?

Osborn. He was what changed. Did his presence have something to do with their onset? Would they grow stronger the longer she stayed? Or was it all coincidence? Would her powers eventually have appeared?

Breena stretched her arms high above her head. Her neck was stiff, and her back ached, but it felt good to be alive. She glanced around the tiny cottage.

Loud whispers echoed in the bedroom, and she knew the three Ursan men were awake. It had seemed so perfect when she'd stumbled upon them yesterday. She kicked the covers off, and began folding the blanket. Breena didn't want to be accused of dawdling. The door opened, and Osborn stepped out of the bedroom. "You're up."

Turning, she made herself busy straightening the blanket. She wanted to avoid seeing his handsome face. Now that she knew he wasn't her warrior, she didn't want to…

She didn't want to still desire him.

Bernt and Torben pushed themselves past their brother, fully dressed and ready for travel. "I didn't think you were coming with us," she said, thrilled there'd be some kind of buffer between her and Osborn.

"I don't want the boys alone in case any more of those creatures come here."

Cold. Logical. "I'm ready," she told him, unwilling to meet his gaze.

After she used the privacy area, the four of them set out after a simple breakfast. Despite the boys' attempts to cajole her into sharing more stories, the camaraderie of the evening before was definitely over.

"How long does it take before we get to the

village?" she asked Bernt after they were well into their walk.

"We can usually arrive by noon," Osborn answered instead.

Some time later she stumbled over a dead tree limb hidden in the brush. Three different male hands offered assistance. She grabbed for Torben's and Bernt's. Osborn's eyes narrowed, and he glared at his brothers.

Around midmorning, they stopped to take a break around an old fire ring obviously used by travelers. The boys ran off for privacy while she plopped herself on a wooden stump as far away from Osborn as she could get.

A large figure blocked the sun. A shadow fell across her lap as she was rubbing her feet. An Osborn-shaped shadow. But she didn't look up. "You've been avoiding me all morning. Why?"

Her shoulders slumped, and instead of feeling lighter that Osborn would soon be out of her life for good, the knowledge weighed on her heavily. She understood his reasons for not helping her, but she wasn't going to make it easy on him.

He wore his longish hair tied back for their trip to town. Black seemed to be his color of choice; he wore it again today. He kept his appearance modest, but there was nothing simple about the huge sword strapped to his side. All together Osborn was devastating to her senses. Never had a man looked so strong, so powerful and so capable to her than the warrior. And right now she needed all of those things. Desperately. How could she not respond to him physically? Emotionally? And now he wanted some kind of explanation about her avoidance of him.

After steeling herself against the pull of his dark brown eyes, she met his gaze. "What do you want from me? I came to you for help. To find my family, to avenge their deaths. You won't give it to me—I can accept that—but I don't plan to sit around and discuss the weather or something with you now."

He glared down at her. "You tried to get your magic to trap me."

"If that's how you want to view it," she told him, her voice tired. If that's how he still thought of her, she'd never convince him otherwise.

"I won't be used. Ever again. By anyone."

"Good for you, Osborn. In fact, go back to your cottage and just seal yourself from the rest of the world. Forget how to live, and die alone because you'll eventually run your brothers off, too. Just point me in the direction of town, and I'll handle the rest."

"I'm taking you," he said between clenched teeth.

She put the uncomfortable shoes back on her feet. "Then let's not waste any more time here. The sooner you discard me at the village, the sooner you can be away from me."

Breena began walking in the direction they were originally headed, and when Osborn's brothers fell along beside her, she let out a small sigh of relief. After her big talk to their brother, she'd hate looking foolish by having to turn around and walk a different direction.

The sun was almost directly overhead when they crested a small hill. Below them a green valley stretched to the horizon, and there, nestled at the bottom, was a village. Having always been kept behind castle walls, the idea of exploring, even for just a few moments, took away the gloom of Osborn leaving her and what she must surely face in the coming days.

"Let's go," she told the boys, and they looped arms and charged down the hill, laughing all the way. Osborn followed behind, his hand never leaving his pack, his gaze constantly scanning around them.

The village was charming; the houses were similar to Osborn's cottage but sanded and painted bright colors. A central road divided the small town, and booths and stalls invited her with enticing smells and beautiful fabrics. She remembered a story her mother once told of a boy made of wood tempted by all he saw in the village. The sights and the smells in town awed the boy, but he was also not careful and lost his money to a crafty fox and cat. The need for caution rang true now more than ever, but so did the lure of all there was to see and explore.

"What do you want to do first?" she asked.

"Eat," both boys replied in unison.

She laughed until Osborn's booming voice interrupted her. "Bernt, Torben, you go along. Breena stays with me."

Torben looked like he might want to argue with his older brother, but the temptation to explore was just too great.

"Back in two hours."

With a quick wave, both boys abandoned her. In a flash they were out of sight, and she felt the heavy presence of their brother at her side.

"I have a little money. It's not much, but it should keep you from stealing anyone's breakfast," he said, his voice almost kind.

Breena smiled despite not wanting to. Why did he have to be nice? She really wanted to dislike him. It would make his leaving her so much easier.

"Thanks," she managed to mumble. This would be the last time she would see him. She'd never dream of him again. Wouldn't let herself. She began to stare at the booths, hoping he'd just leave.

"Breena—" he said, then stopped.

His voice was so raw, so full of yearning, she couldn't help but meet his gaze.

"Breena, I—"

Raising up on tiptoe, she kissed his cheek. "Me, too," Breena whispered in his ear, then she turned from him, and charged into the crowd.

He watched her walk away. Forced himself to spy the back of her blond head until she was swallowed up by the people of the village bargaining for deals at the various stalls lining the dirt-packed road.

Osborn stood searching the crowd for her, but finally turned his back. Breena was gone.

He might as well enjoy himself while he was here. Eat something neither he nor his brothers cooked. Maybe find a woman to drive his thoughts of Breena out of his mind.

The idea of it made him shudder, and he knew thoughts of her would always be close by. His hands turned to fists. He'd tasted something close to perfect. Held her in his arms, felt her soft body respond to his touch, his kisses. Her nipples hardened in his palms with just the barest caress. And she was walking away from him? The berserkergang in him raged, turned protective. Going to find herself another warrior?

Not. Going. To. Happen.

"Breena," he called, but received no response. He was taller than most of the villagers, so it was easy to scan the crowd, but many of the women here sported blond hair. He quickly passed by each stall, bumping shoulders with some, sending others scurrying out of his way. Nothing on the right. He crossed the street and began his search on the left side of the booths. He almost missed the narrow alley between buildings, but something drew his eye.

Maybe it was that his eyes automatically locked on anything blond.

Perhaps it was the glint of the sunlight off a knife blade.

Whatever it was, he turned down the alley to spy Breena, surrounded by three burly-looking men.

"Breena," he called, growing anxious.

That's when he saw the knife at her throat.

A swift chill invaded his arms and legs and his gaze narrowed into a tunnel. Every emotion—all his desire for Breena, the aching need for whatever it was she offered that had lodged in his chest—focused into anger. His berserkergang stirred and in less time it took for the man with his blade at Breena's throat to take a breath, Osborn's Bärenhaut lay around his shoulders with the knife removed from his boot and at the man's throat.

He didn't live long enough to take second breath. The would-be abductor fell at Breena's feet. She screamed, backing away from the body, and the two accomplices rotated to face him. Their eyes rounded in horror, their hands shaking in fear.

Osborn's berserkergang always liked the fear. Thrived on it. The walls around them shook with his growl, and he went after the man closest to Breena. "Dare you harm a woman?"

"Just after a bit of fun. We had no money for the paid women. You can have 'er first."

His offer was the last thing he spoke as Osborn snapped his neck with one hand. He rounded on the last, his knife in his hand. But the berserker hungered for barehanded combat.

"I wasn't gonna do anything. My brother made me come."

The man's crying words didn't slow Osborn from stalking toward him. His prey dropped to his knees, not much older than his own brothers, and Osborn paused.

"D-don't kill me. Please."

His berserkergang forged images of his dead mother and sister. Osborn wrapped his fingers around the young man's throat. "Never touch a woman like that," he ordered, his voice more of a snarl.

The young man shook his head. "No. I won't."

Osborn tightened the grip he held around his neck, watching as his face turned purple and his eyes grew more fearful. "Never harm a woman."

He could only nod in response and Osborn let him go. The alley filled with the man's deep gasps of breath.

Osborn never took his eyes off him. “You live. As a warning. Go.”

“Thank you,” he said, running as fast as he could down the alley and out of sight.

He turned on Breena, who lay on the dirty cobblestones of the alleyway. Her eyes were filled with confusion, and terror lined her soft features. His berserkergang bristled and swelled, at first thriving off her fright. Osborn stalked toward her. Breena shrank away, crawling backward, doing what she could to get away from him. To survive.

The berserker inside him recoiled at the sight of her fleeing. His rage weakened suddenly, a different path from the slow fade his anger usually took. The day before, when he'd found her invading his lake, he wanted her to be afraid of him. Now the idea repulsed him. Made him feel ashamed.

Breena had backed herself into the wall, her eyes darting, searching desperately for a way to escape. He shucked off his pelt, tossed his knife to the side and sunk on his haunches.

“Breena.” His voice still shook with traces of his berserker rage. He closed his eyes, concentrated and forced the *ber* spirit inside him to settle. He'd never battled against his own berserkergang. Had never needed to. He glanced down at Breena. Never wanted to.

He gently touched her arm, the warmth of her skin chasing away the cold his berserkergang always left behind. Osborn watched as she took a deep breath, and forced her back to straighten. He hid a smile, because he knew Breena was girding herself to do battle. With him.

After a moment, she finally met his gaze. Accusation laced her green eyes, and any idea he'd had earlier of smiling vanished.

Breena was looking at him like something unworldly. Despised. It was something he was used to. Only he hadn't realized he didn't want *her* looking at him that way.

Few outside of Ursa understood the nature of his people. One of the reasons they kept to themselves. Most of the inhabitants of the other realms were afraid or relegated them as little more than animals. Things to be feared, yes, but also abhorred.

Osborn's stare never wavered from hers. His expression grew brutal. Distrustful. He wasn't in the practice of guarding his expression, and now was too late to start. But Breena's beautiful green eyes were only filled with curiosity. That full bottom lip of hers curved in wonder.

"What are you?"

Chapter 7

So *this* was her warrior.

Breena had never seen anything so savage. Osborn fought with a ferocity unmatched by anything she'd ever witnessed. The knights who'd pledged themselves to her father prided themselves on their skill with a sword, jousted and battled from the lists at tournaments with precision and pride. But Osborn's raw strength and power during the attack was brutal and ruthless.

Almost like an animal.

The perfect challenge to one who wielded blood magic.

A tide of denial and horror swept over her abruptly. Her knees weakened, and she doubled over. Osborn was at her side, his long stride getting him there in two quick steps. His strong fingers tangled in her hair, soothing her, and her stomach calmed.

"They were going to kill me."

The man beside her only nodded. No words were needed.

"Tell me what you are, Osborn," she urged.

He looked into the distance. "I'm a man."

"You're more than a man, you're something else. Tell me."

"I'm berserker. I fight with the *ber* spirit."

"But how can that be? No one has spied a berserker for years. They've vanished. I almost believed it to be a legend."

"Gone. Forgotten as if they never lived," he said, his words bitter and biting. "I have vengeance of my own to think about."

She shrank away from him.

His sigh was heavy and he rubbed the back of his neck in obvious frustration. "Are you okay?" he asked after a few moments of taut silence.

The man didn't want to care.

But he did.

As if the sun had shot out bright rays to illuminate the truth, Breena knew she had her weapon against Osborn…if she wanted to wield it. She sucked in a deep breath and squeezed her eyes tight in relief. Breena had the weaponry, but it was his need to protect her that made her heart race.

She swallowed past the lump that had lodged in her throat. “Yes. Thanks to you.” She flashed him a grateful smile. He blinked at her, settling on the backs of his heels. Was he surprised? How did he think she’d react? Afraid? He looked over to his side, examining the dead bodies to verify that, yes, they were indeed still dead. He wouldn’t meet her gaze. Osborn *was* afraid that she’d reject him or be frightened by him.

She gripped his arm, giving him a squeeze. Her own magic hadn’t been wrong to draw her to this man. He *had* to be the one who’d help her reclaim Elden.

But the man maintained a real aversion to the notion that he was being used for his sword. Something had made him hard and suspicious, and she was going to find out. Her mother often complained of men stifling their emotions and that half the time a woman needed to come along and give them a good pop just to release the pressure. Osborn seemed to be holding himself tighter than a sealed drum. Maybe what he needed was for her to give him a good figurative smack.

Maybe he needed her just as much as she needed him.

Now to get him to aid her without him knowing. She searched her mind for ideas, quickly discarding and refining until she hit on a scenario Osborn just might agree to.

She brushed the hilt of his sword. "Teach me."

He glanced down at her fingers wrapped around the handle of his sword, then up at her. "What?"

"Teach me what you do."

Osborn shook his head. "It cannot be taught to a woman. At least, I don't think so. There were never any women with the berserkergang."

"Then teach me to fight. I've never seen anything like what you just did. You were strong when you fought the creature in the lake. I doubt any man could walk away from that battle as you did, but in the alley you were invincible." What was it her mother always said? That there was nothing wrong with spreading a little flattery when it came to a man?

At least he seemed less…unrelenting.

"There will be other men bent to attack me now that I'm out on my own. I have to be able to protect myself."

Her fingertips bumped into his, and he jerked. *Good.*

"You won't be my warrior, I can accept that, but at least give me a chance. Surely there are methods I could learn from you—how to use a knife… something. Anything, Osborn. I have to find my people. To avenge." *To survive.*

His shoulders slumped. *Yes, she was wearing him down.*

He stood, towering over her, then extended his hand to help Breena to her feet. “I don’t wish to talk in this place of death.”

She glanced over at the two dead bodies and then quickly looked away. “What about them? Are we going to leave them here?”

“Vermin like that? Anyone who’d prey on the helpless, especially women and children, deserves nothing less. This is where they belong.”

After wiping his blade, he slammed his knife home in his boot scabbard. Reaching for her hand, he guided her toward the entrance. He scanned the scene past the alley, keeping her in place against his back. A protective move, and she allowed herself a small bubble of hope.

Apparently satisfied no one would witness their escape, he pushed them forward, joining the bustling crowd. Osborn routed her in a direction leading away from town, winding through the streets of the village, and avoiding contact with strangers. She tried to reclaim her earlier enthusiasm for this visit before she’d been attacked, wanting, *needing,* something normal. Maybe if she concentrated on the wares at the various stalls and booths. But Osborn led her past each one, refusing to pause even at the ones selling delicious pastries and pies, despite their tantalizing smells.

"Pretty lady, over here."

"A ribbon for her, sir?"

But Osborn ignored them all, and kept them walking. Once out of earshot of the townspeople, she couldn't hold her questions in any longer.

"I've heard the berserkers were crazed. Couldn't control themselves when they were…" She didn't know the word. Few did anymore.

"Under the berserkergang," he supplied for her. "And if we couldn't control it, that'd make us poor warriors."

"I could sense it, that berserkergang. You're the most powerful fighter I've ever seen, but you knew who I was and didn't hurt me."

"No, I wouldn't hurt you," he told her softly.

Did she mistake hearing that near whisper of his? *Not on purpose.* "What happens to you after the rage has passed? I've heard berserkers are at their weakest, but you were invincible after the fight."

"Nothing is invincible. The wolves have their silver, the vamps have their sun. I am just a man, but with my Bärenhaut, my pelt, only raw materials of the earth can hurt me. If the battle is long, then yes, I cannot go on without rest."

"And if the battle is short?" she was almost afraid to ask.

"Then I seek the relief only a woman can give." She felt her cheeks warm with embarrassment. As he'd intended her to feel. That was the last question she planned on asking, and she had so many about the man. She suspected most would go unanswered. Was that why she found him so intriguing? That she'd never fully know the story of this berserker?

"What other things have you heard of my kind?" he asked.

So he *did* want to have a conversation. "That women aren't—"

She stopped her words in time. Was she about to actually tell him that?

"Breena?" he asked, using a voice she suspected few had dared argue with.

Something flickered in his eyes. Heated.

"That women aren't safe around berserkers. That they take what they want. Who they want. Make a sport of challenging men with daughters."

He halted and gripped her shoulders, forcing her to face him.

"That rumor's true," he told her, his eyes on her soft lips. He grasped her chin between his fingers, rubbed the tender skin with his callused thumb.

"Do you feel safe with me, Breena?"

She chose not to answer. Breena pulled her chin from his clutch, and they continued down the path.

Not too far on the outskirts of town, a peaceful green-grassed clearing stretched near a quiet river, and Osborn finally stopped. The line of the forest stood only a few steps away, and the fresh pine smell scented the air.

"This is beautiful," she told him, remembering the story of girl who stayed too long in a meadow picking flowers. She'd enjoyed the sun on her face so much that she'd lost her way, finding only a wolf to trust to lead her home.

"It's easily defensible."

"What does that mean?"

"With the river to my back, I only have to defend three sides. The forest can provide coverage for a potential enemy or if I need to regroup."

So many things to know. Where she saw a place to kick off her shoes and run, Osborn saw as a good place for battle. "See? I'm already learning."

Her warrior met her gaze, and the smile on her face disappeared. The fierce passion simmering in his eyes made her swallow. "I will teach you, Breena. But what will I get in return?"

"Wh-what do you mean?"

"Everyone must earn what they eat. What can you offer?"

"Well, I can…" She tried to remember all the important duties she maintained in the castle that could translate to Osborn's home. "I can sew a beautiful tapestry for the cottage. Maybe one depicting your greatest victory," she told him, warming up to the idea.

He raised a brow. "What would I do with a tapestry?"

"The fabric holds the drafts at bay. It will keep the cottage warm at night."

The brown in his eyes darkened. "I want other things to keep me warm at night."

Images of them together, skin to skin as they were at the lake, warming each other with only the heat of their—

"I can carve candles that can light the cottage at night," she rushed out in the hopes of chasing the idea of them intertwined out of her mind. "The candles are bright enough to work by."

"My brothers and I work sunup to sundown. We have no need of candles, we're already in bed when the moon is out."

Osborn seemed so much closer than he had just a moment or two ago. The clean, crisp scent of the woods that surrounded the cottage filled her nose, and her arm felt warmed from the nearness of his big frame. Too near.

"Give me your hand," he told her.

With a reluctance she didn't want to show, she offered him want he wanted. His long fingers engulfed her hand, and he turned it over to examine her palm. He gently rubbed his thumb over a scratch at her wrist. The feel of it sent shivers down her arm.

"How'd you get this?" he asked.

"When I was wondering around in the woods, I fell and landed on a stick."

His fingers glided along her palm, and she found it hard to breathe. "How about this abrasion to the heel of your hand. How did you get this?"

"I was trying to climb a tree for some fruit. The bark wasn't very forgiving."

He brought her palm to his lips, and placed a kiss to her injury. Except nothing on her body was in pain anymore. She'd never felt so…well.

"Your hands are soft. When you cup my cheek, it feels like the petals of a flower against my face."

Those shivers he'd started with his thumb, they were now generated by his words alone. An awareness of him, of his strength and scent and beauty as a man, made her tremble. He placed her hand on his neck, and her thumb began to explore him in tiny circles. The way he encouraged her touch in his dream. Their dreams.

"You don't have the hands of a woman who works to earn what she eats. You do not prepare the meals in your home, do you?"

Breena shook her head.

"Nor do you wash the clothes or even sweep the floor."

An edge to his voice took her out of the soft haze his words had seduced her into. Osborn was trying to prove some point here. She just didn't know what it was.

"You can't cook. You don't know how to do laundry or mending or take care of a house. How will you repay me for my training time?"

"You could teach me those things and then I could do them for you."

"That would take more time and I'm not inclined to waste."

"There's got to be something I can do to get you to teach me," she said, hating how her voice sounded so near a plea.

Osborn lifted a brow. "I wonder what that could be."

Then his gaze dropped to her breasts.

Her breath hitched. Her nipples tightened, and pushed at the rough material of her loaned shirt. An inner warning told her Osborn's actions were far more calculated than only desire. He was challenging her, trying to intimidate her, and make her wary so that she'd back off and not seek the killers who murdered her family. Breena would not be intimidated. She shrugged her shoulders, not realizing until afterward her movements would make her breasts push even more against her shirt.

His eyes narrowed at the changes of her body. He seemed to grow bigger, more tense, if such a thing were possible, right before her eyes. A ripple of want rushed through her. Breena longed for the feel of him. His touch chased everything from her mind but him, and the way he made her feel. Breena forgot to be afraid, to worry and to mourn what she couldn't fully remember but knew was lost.

He reached out a hand and cupped her breast. Filling his palm, molding her to his liking. She gasped when his thumb slid over her nipple in a gentle caress.

"Why'd you come back for me?" she asked, needing to know the answer almost as much as she needed his hands on her.

"This," he said, and he tugged the large shirt down exposing her breast. He leaned down and took it into his mouth. Breena clutched his shoulders at the exquisite feel of his lips on her skin, the warmth of his mouth and the gentle graze of his teeth on her nipple. Her knees felt weak again, and she grasped him tighter, losing her fingers in his hair and rolling her head back to allow him more of herself.

"You taste so good," he said against her skin, and he tugged on the other side of her shirt, giving him free rein to her other breast.

"You feel so good," she echoed.

Osborn made a little growly sound, and he circled the tip of her nipple with his tongue. Warmth and wetness pooled between her legs. This was better...

"What's better?" he asked.

Breena hadn't realized she'd spoken her thoughts aloud. "This is better than in our dreams."

He cupped her backside in his hand. "Because it's real."

Yes. Her imagination could never conjure up anything this frantic or exciting. Yet what would it mean for him? She didn't know much in the ways between a man and a woman, but she'd observed enough to see a man pair himself off with a different maid of the castle every night.

"I'm nothing to him," she'd heard one girl sob to another, "just a body."

That's what Breena would be to Osborn. A bartered body. Someone to steal a moment's pleasure with to forget whatever pain made him so hard and mistrusting. Then she'd be forgotten.

She didn't want this man to forget her.

Breena pushed Osborn away, her wayward senses protesting his leaving. After righting her shirt, she smoothed a hand over her hair. His unruly hair was now free of the leather binding, probably her doing.

His stare never left her face.

"Okay, Osborn. I'll do it for your training."

His face drained some in color, confirming her suspicion that he'd started the intimacy between them to shock her into changing her mind about facing battle. Then his eyes lowered once more, her nipples still tight points and clear against her shirt. His nose flared and he reached for her.

She quickly sidestepped his advance, fluffing the shirt away from her chest. "I will do the mending. I did mention that I could sew."

Years ago, Rolfe had made a vow to the King of Elden. To protect the king's family with his own life if needed. And he would have faced any battle, raised any sword against any who threatened the Royal House, but this—

This wasn't battle, and he didn't face his demise. It was worse than any death. Any pain. Any suffering.

It was a living death. Unremitting agony. A soulless life. Others had gone mad from the threat of it. Rolfe's own fright had kept him clinging to the shadows of the castle. As a guard he knew the best ways to go unnoticed, slipping around Elden, squirreling away food like a rodent. He'd become someone he didn't recognize. A man who valued going undetected over honor. But what was honor and principles here? That had all died with the king and queen.

Maybe the depraved death the Blood Sorcerer offered would be simpler than this pitiful existence. It was easy enough to be caught. Catching the attention of one of the blood minions, maybe steal something in plain sight. He knew some of what happened to those who refused to give their allegiance to the Blood Sorcerer. Drained of blood, used as target practice and blood sport or fed upon by something so hideous the screams started before the feeding even began. But the screams eventually ended.

That's what Rolfe wanted. Needed. What came after the silence.

He'd failed. The king and queen were dead. The three princes vanished, even the sweet princess he'd tried to save now all gone. His heart constricted at the pain. His defeat.

What was his life worth now to Elden? Better to face the end now than to go on living with the failure. He heard voices in the hall.

The Blood Sorcerer sat on the King of Elden's throne. The former king. The body had been removed, but the stains from his blood still covered the floor. One of the castle servants tried to clean up the carnage left by her dying ruler's body, but the sorcerer quickly put a stop to that. He thrilled at walking through the spilled blood of Aelfric. The dead king's pain, the anguished cries, energized the great hall. The sorcerer still felt the traces of Aelfric's fear for his children's safety, and his growing need for vengeance, even as his life's blood drained away, seeping onto the cold stone floor for the sorcerer now to plod through.

A wish for vengeance that would be denied.

Even now the Blood Sorcerer's minions were verifying the deaths of the heirs of Elden.

Leyek entered the great hall and bowed low to him. The sorcerer demanded the same displays one would give royalty. He *was* royalty. Better than any crowned monarch born of birth. The sorcerer had *earned* his right to walk exalted among the people. Killed until he reigned above all others. Drained the blood of many to sit on this gilt-and-jeweled throne.

"One of the scouts has returned, my lord," Leyek informed him.

He unfurled his long index finger. "Only one?"

His minion nodded. "Yes. Your creature is weak. He must be fed before his questioning."

The Blood Sorcerer stood, anger simmering around him. A visible mist. "Then see it done. There are plenty of Elden's citizenry in the storehouses."

"Already done, my lord."

The mist began to dissipate. Leyek had earned his second in command years ago, and was bloodthirsty enough to not let his position weaken. "Good. Which heir?"

"The scout was too weak, but this pairing was after Dayn. Or the sister, I think."

The Blood Sorcerer began to fondle the dark red rubies embedded in his chair. "Let's hope it's the girl, and that she's still alive. I relish the draining."

He closed his eyes and shuddered in anticipated pleasure.

Agonized cries echoed outside. "Good. The feeding has begun. Let me know when he's finished off with his stock. I want to be one with my pet in the questioning."

Leyek nodded. "Very good, my lord."

The Blood Sorcerer gave a disinterested wave of his hand. "Make sure the draining is slow and extreme. My pet deserves a treat."

Something kindled within Rolfe. Some spark… some return to life. The desire to survive.

One of the heirs still lived.

Lived only to be hunted and slaughtered. But Rolfe might be able to prevent their capture. A small, sliver of a chance, yet he'd take it. He'd make himself invaluable. Learn all he could of the blood scouts, and steer them away from the heir they hunted.

Osborn was silent beside her as they traced their path back into town to buy supplies. Silent but certainly not forgotten. Breena had tried, forcing herself to enjoy the freedoms that awaited her. She'd focus on only the good experiences to be had in town, the booths, the food, the newness of it all. She'd forget about the men who dragged her in the alley. Their deaths. She had to put those thoughts aside, and block every painful experience she'd had since Rolfe shook her awake. It all seemed a different lifetime ago. Happened to a different person. *Good.* It was the only way she could face what was next to save her family and her people.

More villagers filled the streets and small groups clustered in front of the more popular booths. A surge of excitement quickened her steps, and soon she and Osborn were among the crowd. Even without the berserker she knew lurked below Osborn's very prickly surface, he was one intimidating man. Tall and broad, there was no hiding the raw strength of him. The shopkeepers, eager for a sale, took a step backward as he approached, and she'd seen several people cross to the other side of the narrow street to avoid accidentally getting in his way. If he were one of her brothers, she'd tell him to remove that ever-present scowl on his face, he was scaring the townspeople. Or maybe it was those dark brown eyes of his that made those around his wary. He was constantly scanning the crowd, assessing the level of threat.

She may have grown up a sheltered princess, but Breena knew that kind of alert wasn't instinctual. Her brothers were fighters after all. No, a man with that kind of guardedness and suspicion was like that because he'd brought danger down upon himself. His own doing.

The tales she'd read as a child always hinted at the softer side of the beast, but Breena suspected whatever soft side Osborn once had, he'd stomped to the ground and then did a little dance on its remains.

A smile tugged at her mouth, and Breena laughed at the foolish image she'd conjured in her head.

Osborn glanced at her sharply, and she laughed out loud. She'd blame her silly behavior on lack of sleep and the bone-deep weariness of her aching body that made her laugh with such little provocation. But it felt good to laugh. He stopped at a booth and she continued on, knowing his eyes would not stray from her for long.

"Do you need help?" the lady asked her quietly, darting a quick glance in Osborn's direction. His attention was on the rope he was inspecting, but it would only be a distraction for a moment or two. His vigilant gaze would be upon them both soon.

"Help?"

"To get away," she explained, her voice a quiet hiss.

Tears filled her eyes, as Breena realized what the woman before her was asking. The shopkeeper was trying to help her, escape from the terrifying man who always kept her in sight. She quickly blinked the tears back. Crying would only alarm the woman further, and draw Osborn's watchful eye. Breena managed to shake her head, overwhelmed by the kindness of this stranger. She'd faced a warrior and battled a creature of blood magic, but it was this one woman's compassion that nearly reduced her to a shaking mess.

The woman's gaze narrowed. "There are rumors of that one. He's a killer. Ruthless."

That's exactly what Breena was hoping for.

"We've struck a bargain," she told the woman who despite her obvious fear of the man, would help Breena if she could.

Osborn had finished his transaction, and had turned his attention back to her. That fierce battle face of his firmly settled.

The woman beside her sucked in a fearful breath. "You're sure?"

Her magic led her to this man. Breena was as sure as she could be.

"I'm here every other day. I've helped other women in the past. Just send me word, and I'll do my best to get you free of him."

Breena shook her head again. The rough fabric of the shirt rubbed at her nipples.

"Actually, there are a few things I need."

If Bernt and Torben thought it was strange to see Breena at their brother's side at the rendezvous point, they didn't show it. They walked together as a group, silent, as Osborn bought additional supplies from the vendor. No one asked what she carried in her package, and she didn't volunteer the information. These men didn't need to know the intimacies of her underthings.

She caught snippets of agitated chatter from time to time.

"Did you hear? They found Unwin and Dudley dead. In one of the alleyways."

"Thieves, the both of them. Surprised it hasn't happened sooner."

No one seemed to mourn the loss. A few days ago, the thought of someone dying, seeing someone killed before her eyes, would have been horrifying. Now she viewed the ruthlessness of others in a far different light, and the death of those who would murder without conscience did not bother her.

At another booth the vendors speculated on a suspect. "Who could have done it?"

"With so many strangers pouring into the village on market day, who's to know?"

Both stall keepers quieted their speculation as she approached with Osborn and his brothers. She couldn't help following her nose to the origin of the amazing scent, and the warrior had indulged her. The tradespeople eyed Osborn with wariness, but not suspicion. Relieved, she smiled at the baker who offered her a sample of the bread. "It smells delicious."

Some time later when the sun was lowering in the sky, Osborn announced it was time to return to the cottage. As they walked up the hill, she couldn't help stealing glances back at the village. So many things to see, and taste and smell. A few days ago she would have yearned for this exact experience.

It was almost dark when she spotted the roof of Osborn's home. The boys quickly set to work, preparing the fire while another returned the pillow and blankets for her to use. Last night, she'd made a pallet on the floor, and apparently that was to be the arrangement again tonight. Probably another one of Osborn's attempts to make her change her mind. It didn't matter, the wooden floor of the cabin wasn't soft, but she slept in front of the warmth of a fire, and her stomach was full.

Osborn walked over to her carrying a large woven sack, usually used to carry potatoes. He dumped it in front of her, and out spilled a pile of socks, shirts and pants. The mending.

"All this?" she asked, before she could stop herself.

Osborn raised an eyebrow. "There is a different deal we could make." His gaze lowered to her breasts, and then moved still lower. To between her legs.

Breena's mouth went dry. Never had a man looked at her so carnally. Acknowledged her secret woman's place with such possession. Her hands began to tremble so she sank them into the bag.

"I love to sew. Mending even more. All I need is a needle."

Osborn's lips twisted as if he were attempting to hide a smile. "In the bottom of the sack. Good night."

She rummaged among the cloth until she found a hard wooden case. Breena tugged it out and opened it to find several silver needles and a small pair of sheers. She reached for a woolen sock, sporting a rip in the heel.

"And, Breena?"

"Yes?"

"I'd like to wear those in the morning."

He turned and left, closing the door firmly behind him. The man apparently didn't believe she could sew. She'd show him; her stitches were always tiny and neat. Osborn the warrior may be something amazing when he fought, but he still only had two feet, and he needed only two socks for the morning. Not the dozens stuffed into the sack.

She was also growing tired of his habit of calling her name after the conversation was certainly over—just to give her another order.

Survive. Yes, that's what she was doing.

Breena closed her eyes and breathed in the woodsy scent that hung in cabin. The smoke from the fire. Once again she'd live through another night. And beginning tomorrow she'd start the second command that echoed in her mind. To avenge.

But first…she picked up a sock and threaded her needle.

A hand to her shoulder woke her up the next morning.

"Wake up."

She squeezed her eyelids tight and rolled away from the voice, sinking deeper into her pillow.

But the voice was insistent. "Time to train."

Breena slowly opened her eyes to see Osborn's familiar strong jaw and firm lips. Kissable. But then her thoughts were always a bit fanciful in that place between sleep and wakefulness. His hair was damp, and his cheek smooth. She reached up to slide a finger across his face.

He jerked back from her touch. Mister Prickly today.

Osborn stood, once again dressed in black, his scabbard slung low on his hip. "There's something for you to eat on the table. I'll be waiting for you outside so you can dress. Bernt and Torben are gathering wood and water. Five minutes."

A hunk of cheese and dried berries waited for her, and she devoured them with pleasure. She'd discovered a smaller pair of drawstring pants in the mending bag last night and, after some trimming with the shears, managed to craft something that didn't drag on the ground. She finger combed her hair, and nearly laughed at the idea of the maids who'd once chosen gowns of silk and fashioned her hair in elaborate styles and adorned her with ribbons and gems.

Who'd recognize her now?

And that was a good thing. She suspected she'd used up most of her allotted time. The impatient look on his face told her Osborn was just about to charge into the cottage and get her. "This way," he said, and guided her to a clearing not too far from the cabin. Breena hadn't discovered this place when she was wandering around his home on that first day. Targets and woven sacks filled with straw littered the area, and Breena realized this must be where Osborn kept up with his training.

Osborn tossed her a stick.

"I thought you were going to teach me how to use a sword," she said, eyeing the sword at his hip. Her gaze slipped lower until she forced it back where it belonged.

He crossed his arms in front of his chest. "Have you ever held a sword?"

Breena shook her head. As if her mother ever would have allowed it. Her brothers wouldn't have dared to let her carry a weapon. Even the adored sons would have been afraid of the queen's ire over that infraction. "No. Never."

"Then that's why you're using a stick. Now, you've seen swordplay?"

She was quick to nod. "My father loved nothing more than to host a tournament. The knights on horseback brandishing their swords with a flourish were a thing to behold."

"It's the flourishing knights who are the first to die."

Breena bit her lip to keep from smiling. Could that have been jealousy? She stood straight instead. "Okay, definitely nothing fancy."

"Hold your sword like you're about to face me in battle."

She lifted her stick. Osborn moved to stand behind her, his big chest warming her back he was so close. The chestnut smell of the soap he must use to wash his hair made her want to breathe in deeply.

He lifted his arm, framing her body with his. "Bend your elbows," he told her, "and bring your arms in close to your sides. The weight of your blade will only increase, and you want your sword to do the work, not your arms."

The new stance did feel more comfortable.

Osborn positioned her arms out from her chest. "See how you've left this entire area open?" he asked, trailing his fingers along her collarbone, and down between her breasts.

Breena could only nod. Her skin turned goose bumpy.

"This is your most vulnerable area. You must always protect it."

She was definitely feeling vulnerable. And she was *really* enjoying her lessons. That hand down between her breasts would be worth a pile of sock mending.

Osborn dropped his arms, but not before brushing the sides of her breasts, her waist and her hips. Breena couldn't help but tremble. "Now turn and face me. Always keep in mind that the first blow is the most important."

"*My* first blow?"

"Doesn't matter," he told her with a shrug. "Either you strike and hit or he strikes and misses—*that's what* determines who walks away. If you strike first, make sure you connect. Otherwise, you are off balance and an easy target for his strike. Which *will* kill you."

Breena began to bristle at that assumption.

"You will be smaller than any man you fight. Not as strong. Those are the facts, Breena. I'm not saying you can't defeat your opponent, but you have to be twice as good as they are. Twice as prepared. You have to find their weakness, and use it to your advantage. What do you think my weakness is?"

Breena ran her gaze along Osborn's broad shoulders, powerful arms and muscled thighs. Heat suffused her cheeks as she imagined her hands following the same path as her eyes—over his firm mouth with the full bottom lip. Down the strength of his brawny chest roped with muscle. The flat tautness of his stomach. And below.

"What's my weakness, Breena?" he asked, his voice less instructional but low and husky.

Their gazes clashed.

"I can't see any."

"Then you're wrong. I'm tall, so that leaves my legs exposed. I'm big, so once I'm off balance… that's a disaster. And I'm a man."

Deliciously so.

"And all men are vulnerable in one spot. Do you know what that is?"

She shook her head.

"Between my legs."

She knew what lay between his legs. Couldn't miss the hard male flesh as he stood watching her dress two days ago at the lake. Stood guard, more like. Flashes of what she'd seen stole in her mind at the most inappropriate of times, and refused to be driven out.

"A knee or a good swift kick will bring most men down, and give you a chance to escape. And, Breena?"

"Yes?"

"Trust me, do not wait to see if he falls. Just get out of there."

This mysterious place on a man was growing more and more interesting.

"But most men are protective of that area. You'll really only get just one chance at him, so make it count. Connect."

A twig snapped, and Breena turned her head. Bernt and Torben were crouched behind a bolder, watching them.

"It looks like we have some company," she remarked with a grin.

Osborn rubbed the back of his neck. "Judging by the sun, they've been there for some time."

Breena glanced at him in surprise.

"You must always be aware of your surroundings. What's hiding in the distance. Who's hiding. Where the ground is loose and rocky. Your position to the sun. An opponent with bright sunlight in his face is at a disadvantage. You can lose your footing easily on an uneven field. The time and place of the fight is almost as important as your weapon and skill."

She'd never doubt her magic again. Her powers had provided quite a warrior.

"What about our two spectators?" she asked, angling her head in the boys' direction.

His face turned grim, and his shoulders slumped as if weighted.

"How old were you when, uh, you became responsible for them?" she asked.

"Fifteen, maybe fourteen. It seems like a different life—" his voice was a tired sigh "—the childhood I had was something distant. As if it didn't happen, and was just a story like those stories you enjoy telling."

When her brothers turned fifteen, the king rode with them daily, supervised their study in the classroom and on the mock battlefield. What kind of men would her brothers have turned out to be without the guidance of their parents? Her heart constricted for little Micah. Still so young, and with no one. She swallowed past the lump in her throat.

She had to get to him. Find him soon.

Breena remembered why her magic drew Osborn to her, as well. He definitely needed her, and so did his brothers.

"Maybe you can ask them to join us," she suggested, her voice light as a gentle wind, so her proposal wouldn't seem so monumental.

Osborn stared at her for a few moments, but his thoughts were not on her. With another of those heavy sighs, he whistled. The two boys stood, appearing plenty guilty and a little worried.

"Do you want to learn how to fight?" he asked.

Two heads nodded enthusiastically.

"Grab a stick."

Bernt gave her a tentative smile when he

stepped beside her, stick in hand. "Thanks," he whispered.

"He knew it was time. He just needed a push."

"If the courtly manners class is over, we'll go back to sword fighting," Osborn called loudly.

There. That's how she remembered her brothers teasing and talking with each other. It was good to hear, and her heart lightened for the first time.

That evening, Osborn led three exhausted would-be warriors back to the cottage. The night air had turned chilly on their walk, and once inside Breena removed the protective metal screen on the hearth, stirred the embers and added a log. Then she sank onto the rug before the fireplace, closing her eyes as she went.

Even Bernt and Toren stumbled to the bedroom, too tired to eat—an occurrence he'd never seen once since his brothers entered their second decade of life. They were on their own, but Breena…that was a different matter. She was unused to this kind of physical activity, and while he knew he must push her, she didn't have to suffer.

With quiet steps, Osborn crossed to the kitchen and began cutting up an apple. He grabbed a piece of the dark rye bread he'd bought at one of the village booths after Breena had remarked that the wares smelled particularly delightful.

Breena lay in a ball on the rug, a strand of her blond hair across her cheek. Dirt smudged her forehead, and her soft skin was pink from her exertion of the past several hours.

And he'd never seen anything more desirable.

The mystical woman who floated into dreams as he slumbered was ethereal and perfect.

The Breena in real life was far from perfect. Her nails were ragged from her wandering in the wilderness. Her palms growing callused from her work with a stick and finally a sword. And although he knew she was raised to be a gentle lady, he suspected a temper, only needing an excuse to flare, lurked beneath the surface....

Osborn wanted to give her that excuse. To be exactly who she was meant to be. And very definitely have the freedom of *his* body. Explore him until her curiosity ran out and his took over.

He'd spent hours of his daytime thinking on this woman who haunted his nights. Now, after meeting her and touching her supple skin, kissing her inviting lips and holding her welcoming curves against him, he knew she would torment him forever.

She burned to avenge her family. In many ways, she was not unlike him. Only the thought of killing the butchers of his family kept him sane. That and knowing he must keep his brothers alive.

Was he doing the right thing in training her?

He didn't even have to search for the answer. It was a quick no. He thought of his mother and his little sister. If they had been the ones to escape and were alone and doing whatever it was they could to see another day, he'd hope someone would help them. Breena needed his help, and all Osborn knew how to do was fight. So he had to train her.

He slid down next to Breena on the floor. The rug was more comfortable than he'd expected and the fire warmed his cheeks. She stirred beside him, scooting closer to him in her sleep. Osborn gently shook her on the shoulder, and her eyelids fluttered open.

"I brought you something to eat."

"Too tired," she said, closing her eyes, and resting her head on his thigh. The berserkergang roused, but he willed himself not to react.

He smoothed the hair away from her face, not wanting to move, but knowing she had to take care of herself. "Eat just a few bites. Tomorrow will be even harder, and you'll need to keep up your strength. Come on, I'll feed you."

With a groan, Breena pushed herself into a sitting position. She stretched out beside him touching hip to hip, shoulder to shoulder and thigh to thigh. He felt his body harden at her touch. She smelled of warm breezes and hard work. The scent was heady.

Osborn reached for a bit of apple. "Open."

Breena dutifully opened her mouth. The first time she didn't argue. Or raise some kind of a counterpoint. Or make some kind of difficult suggestion.

She doesn't challenge you when she's in your arms.

Oh, yes, she did. It was just a different kind. One he relished.

He managed to get three more bites fed to Breena, then her eyes drooped again, and he knew her body demanded sleep over food. Her head slumped on his shoulder. He shifted his arm to get her into a more comfortable position, and she snuggled close against him.

Why the hell had he done that?

Feeling the softness of breasts pressed against him was agony. His cock hardened, and he made it all the worse by caressing her arm and sinking his fingers into her long hair.

"That's nice," she mumbled into his chest. "Feels good."

He should go.

Right now.

He should stand, settle her against the pillow and never think of doing something so stupid like being this close to her ever again. Breena was too much of a temptation. Especially because she'd made it clear she'd rather stitch up a pile of socks before crawling between the sheets with him. Oh, Breena desired him, but she didn't *want* him. And for some reason, desire wasn't enough.

He should go.

Right now.

Breena wrapped her arm around his waist, seeking his warmth. Seeking him.

Maybe he could just lay here with her for a few minutes more.

Chapter 8

Breena woke up warm and so, so comfortable. Which was completely ruined by the glowering, accusing brown glare coming from Osborn. With no berserker change in sight, the rage tightening his face had to be all him.

"What's wrong?" she asked.

"You invaded my dream last night."

She scrambled away from him, shaking her head. "No, you told me to stay away."

"You were there. Kissing me. Touching me. Feel me, Breena. Feel what your dream did to my body. Give me your hand."

It sounded like an order, but it was still a choice. What had she done to him? Curiosity…it had ruined many a princess. It would probably ruin her, too. She placed her hand into Osborn's outstretched palm.

She met his gaze as he tugged her hand downward. "Feel me. Feel what you do to me."

Do not… Did.

He placed her hand between his legs. "Feel how hard my cock is for you."

The word sounded lustful. Sensual. Lascivious, and she wanted more and more. He wrapped her fingers around the hard ridge of him. Her body got that hollow, achy feeling again. She needed something, and knew Osborn could give it to her.

"Touch me like you did last night," he urged, his voice barely more than an aching groan.

"Show me," she told him, wanting to learn how to give him pleasure. How to keep that aching sound for her in his voice.

"Slide your hand under my pants. Yes, that's it."

Her fingers smoothed over the hard ripples of the muscles lining his stomach, down over the hair at the base of him. With a tiny thrill, she gathered Osborn's cock into her hand. He was long, and very hard, and yet his skin was smooth. His muscles tensed as she explored the length of him.

"That's it. More. Like last night. Up and down."

Breena walked her fingers up and down the length of him.

"You were perfect in my dream. As if you knew exactly how I wanted it before I even told you."

With another groan, Osborn stilled her hand.

"Did I hurt you?" she asked alarmed.

He gave a strangled little laugh. The room was filled with the harshness of his breathing. He opened his eyes. "It really was my own dream. That's why you knew exactly how I wanted your touch."

She nodded, and waved her free hand. "See, I didn't use my powers. There's no trace magic."

"What?" he asked as he slowly removed her hand from his body.

"There'd be some kind of residue, an energy all around us." She felt her face drain of color. "Oh, no. I used my magic at the lake when we fought those blood magic scouts. I have to get there."

Breena shoved her feet into her shoes, and raced for the door, Osborn a step behind her. Once outside he took the lead, running along the path until the lake came into sight. She waved her hands, alarm coursing through her. "It's still here. Not much, but I can still feel it. Those monsters will be able to follow it to us. To the cottage. To the village. That's how they probably found me in the first place."

"Can you disguise it? Make it go away?"

"I never learned how. My powers weren't this strong back at El—er, home. My energy came from fear and anger. We'll have to blanket it with something good. Happiness."

She glanced over at Osborn, his face bleak.

"This is going to be tough." Not much happiness there.

"Come here, Breena."

Why was he always asking her to go to him? She was getting tired of being the one to do the moving. She shook her head. "If you want me, you come to me." Besides, she had to discover a solution to this problem.

Breena realized what a huge mistake she'd made by offering that kind of challenge to her warrior. Osborn's eyes darkened. His lower lip grew more full, and curved into something that might be considered a smile on anyone else, but on him, it could only be considered predatory.

"I will," he told her, his voice filled with determined intent. His steps toward her were driven and steadfast. He never dropped her gaze.

Don't back up. Don't back up.

He only stopped when the softness of her breasts grazed his broad chest.

"Do you know what else you did to me in that dream I had with you last night?"

"It wasn't me doing it."

"It will be." Osborn's thumb traced a path along her lower lip. An overwhelming urge to lick his skin, taste him, took her over. She felt hollow inside. Achy.

"Your nipples did exactly what they are doing now. Hardening. Begging for my touch. My mouth."

She shook her head. "It wasn't me."

"It will be," he promised again against her lips. His mouth took over, his tongue pushed inside and she met him with her own. Twining and dueling again and again. She couldn't breathe. Her heart raced. Breena grabbed his shoulders, needing the solid strength of him to remain steady.

She'd never felt this way before. Never responded to anything with so much intensity or reacted so strongly, hungrily. Osborn made her feel alive and warm and grasping for something more.

"What are you doing?" she asked.

"You said we needed to change the energy in this place. We are."

She *so* wanted that to make sense. To continue what they were doing.

"Take your shirt off for me, Breena. I hate seeing you in something that ugly."

Osborn was so big and strong. As a berserker, he could take anything he wanted. Even her.

That's why he always asked. Asked her to go to him. Her warrior didn't want to take; he wanted what would be freely given.

And right now he wanted her shirt. Off.

No man had ever seen her undressed and exposed in that way. Osborn had plenty of opportunity two days ago in this place while they were both naked and battling a creature of blood.

But this was different.

Freely given. Breena gripped the hem of her shirt and then paused. What if he didn't like what he saw? If he found her form undesirable? She fiddled with a loose thread on the borrowed tunic. Of what she'd observed in the castle, the knights never complained of a woman's naked body, always clamored to see more. And Osborn hadn't looked away in that secluded clearing outside of the village.

He'd wanted more.

After stealing a deep breath, she grabbed the bottom of the shirt and tugged it over her head. She tossed the garment out of the way of the water, and straightened her back. Almost daring him to dislike what he saw.

His gaze lowered, and his face tightened with longing. "You are so beautiful," he said, his voice filled with a kind of agonized need. He cupped her breasts, molding them to his hands. His thumbs caressed the tips into tight points. With one arm, he gripped her hip and hauled her off her feet, up against his body. The hard ridge of him, heated and full, surged against the bare skin of her stomach.

He ducked his head, capturing her breast into his mouth.

She moaned deep in her throat when his teeth gently grazed her nipple.

"More?" he asked against the fullness of her breast.

Breena could only nod.

With obvious reluctance, Osborn let her slide down his frame until her feet touched the ground again. He swept off his cloak, and spread it on the green grass. "In my dream, you shared all of your body with me."

She sucked in her bottom lip, toyed with it with her teeth. "It really wasn't me."

"I want it to be."

She wanted it, too. *Want.*

He leaned close. "Make it be for me."

His warm breath sent a ripple of sensation down her neck. Her fingers shook as she reached for the drawstring keeping the baggy pants in place. It should be awkward to remove her clothes in front of a man who just a while ago she thought would kill her. Now it seemed the most natural thing in the world.

With a jerk, the pants loosened around her waist, and with a shimmy of her hips, the material slid slowly down her thighs.

Osborn's eyes followed their progress.

Breena kicked the pants aside, now fully bared to his eyes. And to his fingers. His lips. His tongue.

He reached for her hand, and drew her down with him to the cloak, its soft material protecting her naked back from the twigs and rocks on the ground. After cupping her breasts one last time, he allowed his hands to explore. His fingers trailed down over the curve of her stomach and along her thighs.

"So soft. Your skin warms to my touch."

Yes, she wanted his hands everywhere on her.

Osborn stretched alongside her, his mouth finding her collarbone, moving along its path until he discovered a place below her ear that when he kissed it, her entire body shivered. He groaned at her response.

"Do you like that?"

So much she wanted to do it back to him. "Yes," she told him, her voice drawn and tight to her own ears.

Osborn added his tongue.

Wetness rushed where her thighs met. Her whole body seemed to be curving toward him, craving more of what he could give her. She lifted her knee, and ran the tips of her toes down his molded calf. She gasped when his fingers sank between her legs, the feeling of his gentle invasion exquisite.

"You're so wet for me." His voice was little more

than a growl. With a swipe of his tongue to her earlobe, Osborn began to slide down her frame. Stopping to give a gentle nip to her breasts, and he continued lower.

He tasted the skin under her breasts, circled her belly button with his tongue. Went lower still.

"What are you doing?" she asked.

"Changing the energy."

She felt his warm breath on the curls between her thighs, and she began to shake. He nudged her knees farther apart, exposing her woman's body to his gaze.

"So slick for me."

With one tiny kiss, her every muscle locked. His head descended, and he licked. Her moan filled the clearing around the lake, echoing off the trees.

"I love to hear your pleasure." Then he gave her more. He laved every part of her, and plunged his tongue within her. Every muscle, every part of her that could feel, tightened and narrowed, just waiting for more of his touch.

He began to seek inside her with his finger. The tip delving where she ached to have him fill her.

"So tight."

"That feels so good."

"It's about to get a whole lot better." He lowered his head again and began to suck where her sensations seemed to be the most centered. And her world burst.

Breena dug her fingers into Osborn's shoulders as crest after crest of pleasure slammed her senses. Her cry sailed up to the trees and she arched herself toward him until the amazing sensations died away.

With one last kiss, he rolled to his back beside her, and stared up at the sky.

She rolled toward him, draping her arm over his chest, and cuddled as close as she could. She'd remember this forever.

Osborn tensed when she began to play with the fine hair covering his chest. "You've never done this before, have you?"

Breena shook her head. "That was incredible. You made me… I felt… It's hard to find the words."

She expected Osborn to bask in her praise. Encourage her for more. If anything, his expression grew grimmer than when they'd first returned to the lake.

"Before the invasion of your home, what was your training? What were you meant to be?"

"Be? I don't understand what you mean."

He pushed her hand away from him, and braced himself up on his elbow so he could look down at her, not up. "You're not a servant, or someone who works out in the field. We've already established that. You're something more. You're meant for something. Some*one*. You're a virgin, aren't you?" His tone sounded accusatory, like he suspected she kicked small animals for fun.

Unease settled just below her heart. She nodded, confirming his question. Breena didn't like the direction this conversation seemed to be taking. She didn't know what she was hoping for after an experience that was so intense and personal for her—maybe a hug, but certainly not an interrogation.

Osborn scrubbed his hand down his face. "Should have known. You had that wholesome look about you."

Wholesome?

Men didn't teach women battle skills they found…wholesome. It was a loathsome word.

"You're meant for another." His words were low, spoken into the ground.

"What?" she asked, not sure she heard him correctly.

He aimed his gaze somewhere in the vicinity of her forehead. "Get dressed. You're meant for another. Not me. Never me."

Breena snapped her legs together. A wave of embarrassment and confusion shuddered through her. "You're not making me leave you?"

His breath came out in a heavy sigh. "No, you'll learn what you need to, and then I'll send you on your way."

Relief chased away the confusion, but the

embarrassment still warred inside her. She reached for her discarded pants, and quickly stepped into them.

"And, Breena?"

They were back to that. "Yes?"

"Remember the warning I first gave you?"

Maybe. Which one? There were so many.

She nodded instead. Seemed a safer response now that he was back to being so prickly.

"Don't be alone with me. I don't want my touch to defile you."

Tears filled her eyes, but she quickly blinked them back. "How could what we just shared be defilement?" His caresses had brought something out in her. She felt connected to him. Intimate.

He obviously did not feel the same way.

Osborn finally locked his eyes on her. Her lips. Her breasts. Between her legs. Then his gaze clashed back with hers. Hunger and desire and passion so carnal and raw blazed in the brown depths. "What I want to do with you, yeah, you'd definitely come away defiled."

And she bet she'd have a smile on her face, too. Turning her back to him, she tugged the shirt he hated on her back in place. What did he want her to wear? They were shirts *from* his household.

"And, Breena?"

And again just to make sure she was truly

flustered. Now it was her turn to sigh. "Yes?" she replied sweetly.

"Stay out of my dreams."

"I wasn't in your dreams," she told his retreating back.

After the morning chores, Bernt and Torben met them on the practice field. Osborn paced across the grass, once more the stern and frightening man she'd woken to days ago.

"Balance is the most important aspect of your fight. Once you lose your balance you lose the opportunity to protect yourself, defend…and lunge, your offense. And then you die."

He pointed to three large round stones each with a plank of wood beside it. "Place the wood on the stone and step on. Balance until the sun is directly overhead."

Osborn stalked away and both Bernt and Torben shot her accusatory looks. Breena just shrugged. They knew their brother didn't need any actual real provocation to be grumpy.

The three of them did as they were instructed. Balancing didn't seem too hard. She'd seen plenty of dancers at the palace, and one even walked along a rope suspended between two chairs. Fifteen minutes in and she hated those dancers, and knew the rope balancer had to be a fake. She fell off her plank over and over again. At least she was having better luck than the two boys. They spent more time on their backs than they did standing on their plank. By the time Osborn returned, she was hot, sore and really, really anxious to grab her stick so she could whack him with it during their mock swordplay.

He tossed each of them a green apple and a pouch of water. "Water first."

Despite the fact that their backsides must be sporting a permanent imprint of the ground, Bernt and Torben laughed and teased each other while they ate. Osborn wouldn't look at her, and even though she was surrounded by three other people, Breena felt the loneliest of her life.

Their taskmaster couldn't have given them more than ten minutes of rest. The core of her apple had barely shown itself when he had her up and holding a sword. A real one this time, no sticks. Maybe he'd suspected she'd been entertaining dark thoughts with that stick.

"Take it out of the scabbard," he told her.

She slid the blade from its holder, the sun glinting off the silver edge. There was nothing ornate about this weapon. No jewels encrusted on the hilt, no elaborate carvings marring the blade. A simple weapon. So unlike those of her father and brothers.

"It was my first sword," he told her. "Take good care of it."

And even though she looked up to meet his gaze, Osborn never lowered his eyes to meet hers.

"Thank you," she said. The steel in her hands meant something to the man who'd given it to her. She'd always protect it.

He shifted to face all of them. "In a surprise attack, the fatal blow is often struck before the victim's sword is even drawn. The rest of the afternoon, I want you to practice pulling your sword from its scabbard. Quickly. Quietly. Over and over again until it's second nature to you. You should be able to do this in your sleep. One day you may have to."

For hours they honed this particular skill. She stood still, and pulled the sword from the scabbard; while running, with her scabbard at her side, she pulled the weapon out; when the scabbard was beside her on the ground, she unsheathed the sword. Breena performed the maneuver until it was perfect. Then Osborn instructed her to switch sides and use the hand she didn't favor.

"If you're injured, you may be able to fight off your aggressor."

Every muscle of her body ached by the time Osborn called a halt sometime before the late-afternoon chores. If she thought she was sweaty and dirty after the balance torture Osborn had conceived, she wouldn't be fit to sleep in a stable tonight. She followed him back to the cabin, barely able to hold her sword and scabbard, but not about to ask Osborn for help.

What she would seek his aid in was finding a bar of soap. His lips firmed and that hungry look returned to his eyes when she told him she wanted to take a bath.

"Naked?" he asked.

"That's generally how it's done. How do you wash off?"

She watched as he swallowed slowly. "I usually hop into the lake."

Breena shook her head. "Probably should avoid that place, now that the energy is less…magical. It's too bad you don't use a tub. Sitting in sudsy warm water in front of the fire is one of life's real pleasures."

Osborn looked like he wanted to be anywhere but in this conversation. Too bad. "I'll just grab a basin and wash off in back. Soap?"

"In the cabinet under the window."

"Thank you," she told him with a smile. "No one comes outside," she yelled, so the boys would know to stay inside the cottage. When had she become a yeller? Since meeting up with a family of berserkers, the rage must be rubbing off on her.

The water she'd pumped into the basin was cold, but she knew it would feel fantastic against her hot and sticky skin. The soap, however, was another matter. It smelled like Osborn. Warm chestnuts.

She breathed it in deep, rubbed the soap between her hands until she built a lather, then began running the smell of him all over her body.

Osborn spent the rest of his day wondering about her bath. How she took off her shoes. Her shirt. Her pants. How the fading sun must have glinted off her naked skin. Her hair. He imagined wetting her skin with a sopping cloth, grasping his soap and rolling it along her arms. Over her breasts. Down her stomach. Between her legs.

He envisioned stepping behind her, shedding his clothes and standing before her naked. He *felt* the slick soap and her soft hands along his chest, over his back and gripping his cock. He was in performance mode in record time. She'd slide her hands up and down the shaft of him as she slid her tongue into his mouth. The movements of her hands and mouth mimicking one another. She'd rinse away the soap and sink to her knees. Kiss the head of his cock, tongue the shaft, then slide him all the way into her mouth.

He groaned, nearly coming with the erotic visions. He was going crazy. Osborn had to get her out of his cottage. His life.

But how could he when he wanted her more than almost anything in his life?

He found her later that night, curled on her side in front of the fire. The blanket lay at her feet and he crouched down low to tug it back over her slim frame. Her hair was still damp, but would soon dry before the fire. She shivered, and he worried that she might be cold. Rolling to his side, he fitted her back against his chest. The way her soft curves formed to his body was sweet, sweet torture. One he'd gladly endure over and over.

Breena smelled fresh and clean, and…a little like him. His soap. Possession arced through him, and he curved an arm around her waist. She snuggled toward him in her sleep as though it was natural. Where she should be.

He buried his nose in her hair, the delicate strands sliding over his cheek. Breena shouldn't smell like a man. And he shouldn't be holding her. Wanting more. Needing more. But he'd steal just a few moments. Then he'd pick himself up and go to his bedroom and shut the door. Firmly.

Chapter 9

Breena imagined a door in her mind. Two doors. The second door was new. Menacing. While the first stood familiar, opening that door and walking through had been forbidden to her. She went to it, anyway. Leaned against the closed entry. She longed to go inside. Days had passed since she'd last crossed the threshold and found pleasure. And passion.

But she could not go in.

She turned to the second portal. The entrance was ornate while the other gate was plain. Time-worn carvings in the ancient Elden language adorned the mahogany door. Jewels and rubies, sapphires and diamonds, were embedded in the knob. It should be the most desirable doorway in the world. Instead, she looked again at the simple entry, but that was not her path. That way had been barred to her.

Steeling herself, she gazed once more upon the door that should be inviting. A crimson haze seemed to surround it on all sides. The color of blood. Breena didn't want to go inside. Didn't want to know what lay beyond once she turned that bejeweled knob.

Yet this was her destiny.

Her fingers shook as she reached for the handle and turned. A film of oppressive hate dropped over her, smothered her. Her legs buckled, and she wanted to turn back, but knew she couldn't. Steeling herself, Breena stepped inside.

She was in the great hall of her home in Elden. Beautiful tapestries hung on the walls, and fat tapers illuminated the room, just like always. But instead of the friendly chatter of people, the bustle of the servants and the laughter of the king and queen, she heard only agony. The wailing of the wounded. The fearful cries of those left behind and being rounded up by creatures of unimaginable horror. The smell of blood was heavy in the air. It sickened her, but not as much as the sight of her people, dead and dying on the cold stone of the castle floor.

Breena reached to pick up her skirt to rush to

their aid, but found she wore pants instead. The outfit of a boy. Strapped to her waist was a sword and scabbard. Her fingers sought the timepiece she wore around her neck. She examined the gift her mother had given her at the age of five. A sword was stamped into the face, such an odd symbol to entrust to a little girl. Breena slid the sword out of its scabbard. It was identical to the image on her timepiece.

She *was* on the path of her destiny.

The queen. She thrust the sword in its scabbard, and raced across the room, avoiding the pools of blood and the dead that she could not help. She ran until she reached the dais upon which her parents always sat during the formal times at Elden. She found them strapped to their thrones, a mockery of their honor. More blood flowed at their feet. Thickening.

They were dead. A slash at both their throats. The pain of it so great she sobbed.

Something warm and soothing patted her shoulder in her dream. On instinct, Breena drew her sword quickly and with intent. But no one stood behind her. She returned her sword and braced herself to look at her parents one more time. One last time. They'd each managed to work a hand free from their bonds. They'd died with their fingers intertwined.

Tears began streaming down her cheeks. So

many. Too many to wipe away. But someone gently dabbed the moisture away, and soothed her with a soft whisper. "Sleep, Breena. No more dreaming."

She followed the voice out of her dream. Warmth enveloped her, and she crushed herself toward the soothing strength. And she followed the voice's command and went to sleep without dreaming further.

Breena woke up with her memory restored.

Osborn watched Breena sleep until the birds began to sing. Her sob had jerked him awake. She still lay in his arms, but she thrashed about and she began to cry. He'd never seen a woman cry before. He'd never expected it of Breena, who'd proved she could take as much training and work as a young man learning the ways of a warrior.

Her tears did something to him. Made him feel weak. Made him want to fix or kill or change whatever made her cry. Instead, he could only cradle her to his chest, wipe her tears and try to soothe her with his voice. She finally calmed and settled against him. Her breathing eventually turned steady, and he could relax then, but never sleep.

As the sun broke over the horizon, Osborn knew continuing to train her to fight would only prolong her pain. After last night, he couldn't bear to see her hurt any longer. Today was the last market day of the week in the village. Breena couldn't continue to stay with three men. Surely there was some sort of position, something completely safe, that would keep her employed.

The blood scout had not returned. Had not brought reinforcements, and Osborn doubted the creature would be back with the change in energy at the lake. Blood scouts were little more than mindless drones, obeying only limited commands. Osborn's cock grew uncomfortable as he remembered how he and Breena had chased away the trace magic. He shifted his legs to relieve the pressure, and glanced down at the beautiful woman in his arms. She was gently reared. Perhaps she could be a nanny or maybe a companion to an elder in town until he sorted out everything. Found where she belonged.

Why was no one in her family looking for her?

He feared he already knew the answer.

Osborn gently slid his arm from around her waist and, after one last glance, left Breena to her sleep. He quietly walked toward his front door and slipped outside without waking anyone inside. His brothers wouldn't worry; he often left the cottage early to train, or to run or secure and inspect the perimeter of the sacred lands.

Without the three of them, Osborn stood on the border in no time. The village marketers were just opening their booths when he crested the hill. He quickly made his way down the incline. The first stall he sought sold soaps and perfumes and fancy concoctions used to wash hair.

"For you or for your lady?" the saleswoman asked.

"My lady. I mean a lady."

The woman laughed, flashing him a hearty smile. "I reckon if you give her something I've created, she'll be your lady. I make the best soaps in three realms." She popped the lid off a glass container and held it under his nose.

He breathed in soft vanilla with a hint of erotic spice. *This* was what Breena should smell like. Not manly chestnut. "I'll take it. And the shampoo," he told her.

He continued to make his way through the stall, listening to the snippets of conversation, hoping to glean information without having to ask for it. He stopped when he spotted a beautiful green cloak. Breena's eyes turned that exact shade of sage when he kissed her. Osborn suppressed an inward groan. He'd had to have that, too. He pointed to the cloak of his choice.

"Excellent. My wife just finished this yesterday."

A short woman with a toddler on her hip joined them from behind a privacy curtain. She fingered the material and grinned up at Osborn. "I almost didn't want to give this one up, it's so beautiful.

She's a lucky lady. But have you seen the matching gown?"

Osborn shook his head, quickly realizing he was over his head. Sword—yes. Bow and arrow—no problem. Dresses…

"It will leave her arms bare, but with these gold bands, she can cinch the cloak to the dress and pull it around her shoulders if she gets chilled."

And when the woman laid the gown before him, he knew Breena must have it, too. The old pants and shirt didn't do her beauty justice. And although he didn't mind seeing the material stretch across the rounded curves of her ass, this gown suited her far more. In a few moments, the couple had the garments wrapped and Osborn continued on his way.

A gold armband in a stall a few paces down the aisle caught his attention. He didn't know if Breena wore such jewelry in her old life. The odd timepiece around her neck the only adornment that made it with her to safety. But the armband fit what he knew of her now, and he purchased it, too.

Three packages in hand, Osborn had done nothing he'd set out to do. Obtain information. He backtracked to the first stall where he'd bought the scents. "Have you heard any word of battles?" he asked.

Osborn ground his back teeth. He'd meant to ask about positions for a young woman. Not warfare.

The woman's face grew alarmed. "Here?"

Osborn shrugged. "Anywhere in the area."

"You'll want to be hiring out your sword, I reckon by the looks of you. You're a brawny one," she told him with an inspection up and down.

Osborn shook his head. "No, I'm only checking on…a friend."

"I haven't heard of anything, but go to Hagan, the second to the last booth on the left. He sells spices from all over the realms. If a battle is brewing, he'll know about it."

Armed with a true purpose and destination, Osborn weaved through the growing crowd toward the spice man. After he questioned Hagan, he'd go about securing safe employment for Breena, and this time he would not be distracted.

"How is the basil?" he asked the salesman after his other customer left.

"The most aromatic you will find. Here," he said, opening the spice bag.

"Has the price gone up?" Osborn asked, after taking in the pungent, earthen scent of the herb. "I've heard there's been fighting in that realm and the trade routes are blocked."

The spice man shook his head. "Not with basil. Where you need to be concerned about rising costs is with the olive oil. Elden is under siege, and the oldest trees can be found only in that area. I'd buy all the olive oil you can at the moment, you may not be able to find it later."

A chill ran through him. His berserkergang wakened. "Elden?"

"No one can get in, and what news that's coming out is bad. The queen and king dead. The heirs gone, too."

Something satisfyingly elemental burned in his gut. Elden was finally getting its due. He rued that it wasn't by his hand. He'd always taste the regret of vengeance not fully satisfied.

The berserker in him called for his pelt. Maybe he could brandish the fatal blow and send those cold vamps to their deaths.

Osborn felt lighter than he could ever remember. At least since Elden wreaked havoc and took away most of his life. Now to complete his final task.

Breena ached everywhere. Even her ears seemed to hurt, and she didn't know how that was possible. Her shoulders dragged, and it took her longer than usual to make it to her knees and roll up her pallet and shove it out of the way.

The sun shone brightly through the window. Well past their usual practice time. Osborn must have suspected she wouldn't be much use with a sword today. Especially as he was the one who made her this way.

The bedroom door opened, and Bernt and

Torben slunk inside the main room, looking not much better than she felt.

"I don't want to be an Ursan warrior anymore," Torben said.

"Yes, you do," she told him with a smile. "Grab some apples and bread. We can take our breakfast outside. The sunshine will do us some good."

Once outside, Breena raised her face to the sun, allowing its warm rays to heat her cheeks. She stretched, relieving the tightness of her aching muscles. A blue bird flew over their heads, and she smiled.

"You seem different today," Bernt remarked. A small frown formed between his brows. "You're not wanting to leave us, are you?"

It had never really occurred to her that the boys would begin enjoying her in their lives. She'd felt more like an intruder, one who'd broken their furniture and stolen their food. But now she realized they'd miss her when she left, and she'd miss them.

Would their brother?

"I'll have to go sometime. This isn't my home."

"But it could be," Torben told her. "I saw Osborn clearing out some old furniture and crates out of the storeroom. I think he's wanting to make it into a bedroom."

"He doesn't like you sleeping on the floor."

The thought of Osborn caring about her comfort, trying to find someplace better for her to sleep, made her heart leap.

"I do like sleeping in front of the fire," she assured them. "At home, I had a fireplace in my room. And besides, I'm too tired to do anything but just fall down on the floor and go to sleep."

The boys laughed.

"I like it with you here," Bernt informed her.

"Osborn does, too," Torben added. "I can tell."

"He's a lot nicer. He doesn't yell nearly as much."

Really? Because she thought he yelled a lot. All the time.

"And he finally began our training."

"He was already a warrior by the time he was our age, I think." Torben bit his lip. "He doesn't talk much of what happened to our parents and the rest of our people."

She squeezed the boys' shoulders. "I can imagine what he's suffered. Is still suffering. Remember, he wasn't much older than you when he took on the responsibility of two little boys. When you lose those you love, it changes you. But every day seems better than the last."

That was a lie. A comforting adage she so wanted to believe, wanted these boys to believe, but suspected it would never be true. Each day didn't diminish the hurt, only added more time and distance so that it would be easier to forget.

Avenge.

Breena couldn't forget. Something inside wouldn't let her.

The man who was the topic of their conversation entered the clearing. Osborn never failed to make her breath catch. He looked different somehow. Less grim, and with an added resolve. She hoped that didn't mean more balance practice. He'd tied his hair back, and wore the town clothes from just a few days ago. In fact, he carried several large packages in his massive arms.

"Didn't know if you crew would make it this morning," he told them, something similar to a smile curving his lips.

Bernt and Torben quickly scrambled to their feet.

"Ready for more?" he asked, but his eyes were squared on her. "Get your swords, and head out to the practice field. I need to talk with Breena."

The boys raced to get their scabbards and then flew around the corner of the cottage, leaving her alone with Osborn. He carefully placed his packages on a crate that stood next to the front door, and the dream of last night hit her full force. The pain of it. The anguish. Every vivid detail. But mostly the comfort given as she cried.

Osborn had given her that comfort. Wiped her tears. Breena knew that now. He'd soothed the ache in her heart. If only for a few moments.

Avenge.

Only she could not be truly consoled. Not until the need planted in her consciousness had been relieved.

For the first time, Breena felt uncertain around him. Not sure how to act or where to look. Something in their uneasy relationship had changed in the night while she slept. She twisted her hands, then quickly thrust them behind her back.

"I've been to the village," he told her.

"I can see that," she replied, eyeing the packages.

His eyes narrowed, and his gaze scanned her face, brushed over her every feature. He rubbed his hand along the back of his neck, a gesture she'd seen often enough now to know something heavy weighed upon him.

"I think I found a place where you can go," he finally told her, his gaze dropping.

"Go?"

"There's a woman in the village. She fell last winter and has trouble taking care of her home now. You'd have the entire second floor to yourself, and a little spending money."

"What are you talking about?"

"You can't continue to stay here, Breena," he told her with a shrug. "It's not right. Not a woman with three men."

Breena made a scoffing sound in the back of

her throat. "Are you actually going to talk to me about appearances? Propriety?"

He tugged loose the rope that held his hair in place, freeing the strands. There was her Osborn. Wild and untamed. "I'm trying to do what's right for you."

She marched toward him. Breena wasn't about to let him get away with making decisions for her. "By sending me away? We had a deal."

Breena watched him swallow. Then his gaze turned to hers. "You cried last night, Breena. You cried in my arms." His voice sounded raspy and strained.

A lump formed in her throat. The warrior who'd tried not to care about her worried for her. A lot.

"This isn't good for you. You're not meant for this life."

And she was not meant for him, he was saying.

"I don't want to see you grow cynical and so consumed with vengeance nothing will ever be right for you again."

"I'm consumed with vengeance now."

"And it will eat away at you until there's nothing left but hate. I don't want you to end up like… me."

Breena shook her head. "I can't turn it off. My parents are dead. I saw them die. There was so much blood." She covered her face with her hands.

"I didn't even get to bury their bodies. Something calls out to me. I can't let it go."

"How do you know this? Your memory—"

"My memory came back," she interrupted.

She met his gaze, and what he saw in those green depths made him pause. Made his breath hold and his chest constrict.

"Last night I put myself in a dreamhaze. I went back to the night my parents…" She swallowed. "I went back to the night my parents died. I saw the blood. Their blood. The wounds to their bodies."

Her lower lip trembled, and her eyes filled with tears he knew she fought not to shed. "So you see, I do know the pain of losing something. Someone."

He understood that pain. *Lived* it.

"I know that I can't do anything with my life until I somehow fix this. Vindicate the memory of my family. Keep helping me, Osborn. Please," she urged.

Osborn had left the village with plans and so much anticipation. He wanted Breena to follow a different path than the one he'd followed all his life. He was tired. Tired of his own pain and regret and thirst for a revenge he'd had to put off to raise his brothers. The weariness seeped down to his bones, and the little emotion he had left inside ached.

He didn't want Breena to feel this way. To carry

the burden of avenging the dead alone. To live what he lived.

He rubbed his hand at the throbbing muscles bunched at the base of his neck. He didn't understand until this moment how much like him she actually was. She'd always burn with her need to make right what had happened to her family, because he always burned. "I'll help you."

Breena squeezed her eyes tight and her shoulders slumped with relief. "Thank you."

He doubted she'd be thanking him for long.

The rest of the afternoon they spent in training, and Breena didn't utter one complaint about pains or aches or stiffening muscles. She had survived. She'd convinced Osborn to continue helping her and she was grateful. Her magic had drawn her to the man who'd teach her how to fight who or what had killed her parents.

She'd have to dream her past again. Her body began to shake at the idea of revisiting that night of death, but it was the only way she could find the truth. Would Osborn hold her again tonight?

That evening the boys showed her how they prepared dinner while Osborn closed himself away in the storeroom off the side of the tiny kitchen.

"I can't believe we're having to show a girl how to make us dinner," Bernt grumbled, but it was all in good-natured fun.

"Yes, I thought you would *want* to cook for us," Torben added, and they all laughed.

"I'll just show you how to dance in exchange."

Two matching horrified expressions crossed their faces.

Osborn opened the door of the storeroom, and stuck his head out. A faint smile crossed his features when he saw her. "Breena, come here."

There it was. An order for her to move toward him. She'd almost begun to miss them. Almost. But she was too curious about what exactly Osborn had been doing in that tiny space. She wiped her hands on a dish towel and moved toward where Osborn waited.

"I, uh..." he began, and stopped.

Was Osborn nervous? Breena hid a smile and angled her head inside the place Osborn had kept himself so busy. The store area was small to be sure; four of these rooms would fit inside her bedchamber at Elden. The walls stretched bare and there was nothing on the floor except a tiny blue rug, the color of the blue flowers that grew around the cottage. Not the kind a man would choose for himself, but exactly what a man would buy for a woman. Now she knew what had been inside one of those mysterious packages.

"Nothing much will fit in here but a mattress, but it will be private and all yours, Breena. If you want it."

Osborn's voice was solemn, and she knew he offered her more than just a tiny space inside his cottage. He was offering a place in his life. She nodded her head. "I do want it."

"I have something else for you." There was that smile again. Who knew her berserker warrior was such a gift giver? He came back carrying a small package. She hadn't noticed this one earlier today. She untied the twine and the rough cloth fell away to reveal two glass bottles containing mysterious liquids.

"It's shampoo and soap," he told her.

Breena would have expected cleaning oil for her sword or a new knife, not something so distinctly feminine. She quickly popped off the cork, and inhaled the delicious scent of vanilla and alluring spices.

"Thought you might tire of smelling like a man."

She replaced the cork, and hugged his gifts tight to her chest. "I can't wait to use these. Tonight."

Heat and hunger for her sharpened the features of his face. She lifted up on the tips of her toes, and kissed him on the cheek. "Thank you."

"You're welcome." And there was a promise in his voice that made her stomach quiver.

After dinner, she raced to the small clear spring not too far from the cabin. It wasn't the lake, but it was certainly private. A fact she'd announced to all the berserker men earlier. The spring was hers.

She grabbed the washbasin and filled it with the clean spring water warmed by the sun and wet her hair. At home, she'd always used the floral soaps and scents her mother preferred, but what Osborn had chosen suited her infinitely better. She popped the lid and breathed in deeply of the scent he'd purchased for her. The soft sweet smell of the vanilla combined with the zest of faraway places. This was what Osborn liked, and she poured a small amount in her hand, and cleaned her hair. Did he view her as sweet with a touch of spice?

She ran the soap over her breasts, and the tips puckered. Her nipples did the same when Osborn kissed and licked her there. Breena ran the soap over her skin the way he caressed her breasts. She slipped a soapy finger between her thighs, touched where Osborn had kissed with his lips. Licked with his tongue. She gasped as she imagined him doing that again. Of her licking and kissing him.

Breena wanted that again. And more. He'd barred her from his dreams. Would he still?

Osborn hadn't meant to spy on her bath. He'd only needed to grab more firewood but then he heard Breena's gasp. The berserker in him roused, and he raced to ensure her safety. But Breena's cry wasn't that of a woman frightened, but of her deep arousal.

How much agony did one man have to endure? He leaned against the trunk of a tree, forcing his body to relax. Minutes passed, and she rounded the corner, stopping when she spotted him. Her cheeks were flushed, her bottom lip fuller. A fine sheen of water filmed her skin, and she wore only a towel held together loosely over breasts.

Her face reddened further, and he knew. Knew that when she'd gasped earlier, she'd been caressing herself and thinking of him.

He had an answer to his earlier question. Apparently a man had to endure a lot of agony.

"Osborn, the soap you bought for me was… wonderful."

Her voice was husky, like a woman not yet fulfilled. He imagined her sighing to him in those low tones as he drove into her.

She's not yours.

Breena was loved and protected for another, certainly never a man like him. He was once destined to be something better than he was, an Ursan warrior. With all the honor and distinction that rank held. All he could offer her now was a legacy of shame and a life filled with the need for vengeance

Breena's own steps were aimed squarely at that same path. He'd tried to dissuade her earlier.

Try harder.

But how could he when she was reaching out to him? Lifting her shoulder right under his nose?

"It smells different on my skin than it does in the bottle."

The scent of the soaps he'd bought smelled good, but Breena the woman smelled better. He was so close. Too close. He could nip at her shoulder. Run his tongue along that tantalizing curve of her back.

"I have a favor to ask. "

Gods, anything…if he could just keep breathing in her scent. Prolong the torture by imaging how he could curve his hand around her hip, drawing her backward to cup his erection.

She took a deep breath. "I have to go back to dream of my past, to the night of the siege."

He shook his head, and she gripped his bicep. Hard.

"There's still more to learn about that night. I couldn't continue after, well, you know how you found me."

Crying in her sleep.

"When I put myself in a dream, I always envision a door and then I walk right through it in my mind. There's only ever been your door in my mind.

A possessive satisfaction settled into his chest.

"But last night there were two doors. My past and, next to it, yours."

Osborn stiffened.

"They have to be side by side for a reason. I

think it's because when I go through your door to be with you…nothing frightens me."

"It should. *I* should frighten you." What he wanted to do to her body, what he wanted from her, that should all frighten her.

"But it doesn't." She ran her fingers along his jaw. "You would never hurt me. I've known that for a while."

He didn't know it. In fact, she could almost count on him hurting her. It was inevitable. His past. His decisions. *Those* would hurt her. When his brothers were ready, he'd leave this cottage and seek those who killed his family. His plans were not those of a man who would make life easy for a woman. He gripped her fingers to still her touch.

"Remember how we are together in my dreams?" she asked, refusing to let him push her hand away. "How perfect?"

He could make love to her in that fantasy world she created as they slept. His cock hardened at the thought. Yes. He could caress every part of her body. Brand her with his touch. Drive into her as his body demanded. And he could hold her.

Yet no matter how amazing their coupling would be in the dream, Osborn knew he would wonder and crave the real thing until he was mad.

"Those dreams were lies," he told her, his teeth clenched.

"Aren't you even curious?"

Hell, yes, he was curious. Curious if she'd meet his gaze when he joined his body with hers. Ached to learn the feel of her softness as she welcomed him into her. Dying to know—

"Lies," he said again. Just to stay sane.

Her hand dropped and her expression turned sad. "If it makes you feel any better, sometimes those lies I shared with you were the only thing I really looked forward to." Breena turned on her heel and walked away from him

The blood pounded in his head. Those dreams were the only thing that brought anything even approaching happiness into his life. Until he found her sleeping in his bed.

All she wanted was to dream with him. *Be* with him in a dream. How could he refuse?

He reached for her shoulder, his fingers curving into her skin. "I'll do it."

Bernt had given up his bed for Breena. He and Osborn would begin building a new frame for him the next day. It was a tight fit in the storeroom, but after some shifting and one banged-in corner, the bed finally sat in the storeroom for Breena's use.

She kissed both their cheeks. "Thank you so much," she told them, her voice as happy as if Osborn had bestowed on her the rarest of jewels. Somewhere out in one of the realms there was a man who would be giving Breena gifts with gems and gowns and all the things women liked.

But she was his for now.

Breena quickly dressed the bed in warm blankets and pelts. They wouldn't be sleeping before the fire, and she'd need more coverings to keep warm. There also wasn't nearly the kind of room for the two of them on Bernt's old bed. Breena lifted the blankets and crawled to the edge of the bed, which was pushed up against the wall.

"How do you want to do this?" he asked.

Her lips turned up in a grin. "Not a lot of space for you," she said, eyeing the broadness of his shoulders and the length of his legs. When she looked at him like he was the strongest, most powerful man in the world who could best anything, he wanted to be exactly that for her.

"I like it when you stretch against my back," she told him.

And cupped her breast. And fit his cock against her curves. He liked it, too. A lot. And it was starting to show. The bed creaked under his weight as he settled in beside her. Osborn wanted to bury his face in her hair. Lose the nightclothes that separated her skin from his. He settled for draping his arm over the rounded curve of her hip.

He closed his eyes. Forced his muscles to relax. Imagined smelling rotten food to chase away the erotic scent of her. Anything so that he could doze.

"I can't sleep," she whispered to him after a few moments of silence.

"Nor can I."

"Talk to me. Tell me a story."

She wiggled against him, and he quietly groaned. Every one of her soft curves cupped his body. Osborn concentrated on her request, but could come up with nothing. "I don't know the kind of stories you do. No fairies. No wolves hiding in the woods with their eye on a girl in a red cloak."

"Then tell me something real. From when you were a little boy," she suggested.

Osborn tried not to think of those times. Warriors didn't feel sad. They pushed those emotions to the side. Obliterated them. "There's nothing to tell."

"What about a grand party? Tell me about one of those times when you wore fancy clothes and musicians played."

He breathed in the scent of her hair again, and tried to remember. His people preferred a simpler way of life. Little politics, few dignitaries and lords. They were all just Ursan. They prepared for battles, for when their allies called. Few dared to go to war directly with the Ursans. At night they built large fires. Their entire village would talk and sing along with the drums. A smile played about his lips. He'd forgotten about those nights when the elders pointed to the skies and taught how to use the stars for navigation. He'd forgotten about the songs. Osborn should carve a drum and teach his brothers some of the old Ursan songs. Maybe one day his brothers would marry and teach those songs to their daughters and sons, and hope flooded his chest.

For the first time, guilt and pain didn't rush right behind the memories.

"No banquets," he told her, "just families around the campfire."

"Not even marriage feasts? At home we took every opportunity to host a celebration. My father told us the work in the fields and in the trades could be rough and sometimes bleak. It was our responsibility to provide as much joy and brightness as we could to our people."

"He sounds very wise."

Breena nodded. "He was," she said, her voice quiet and low.

"We didn't celebrate marriages openly," he told her, trying to pull her away from thoughts of her dead father…until she forced herself to dream of him tonight.

"You didn't?" Shock and a trace of scandal laced her voice, and Osborn couldn't help smiling again.

"When a man wished for a woman, he'd ask her to seal her life with his. On a full moon, they'd go, just the two of them, into the woods that surrounded our village. There, with only the stars to see, they'd share the vows they'd written for each other."

"That sounds beautiful. And meaningful."

The yearning in her voice made his gut ache. "That's not the kind of marriage you would have?" he asked, needing to remind himself she was for someone else.

"No," she said on a heavy sigh. "My marriage will be of alliance. It will be an honor to serve my people that way."

"And just how many times have you been told that?"

Breena's muscles relaxed against him. "A lot," she confessed. "In fact, my father was to do the choosing the weekend of the attack."

"Do you think that had something to do with it? An angry suitor?"

"More like a disappointed negotiator. I've never even met any of the potential husbands. Less for them to object to that way."

"And what could they possibly have to complain about with you?" He was incredulous at the thought. Breena was perfect. Perfect for hi—

She only laughed. "I seem to remember you complaining a lot about me. The danger I brought. The added expense."

"My socks are nice."

Breena laughed again, the sound of it thrilling,

like he wanted to make her laugh again and again. Forever.

"Stick to fighting, Ursan. That kind of compliment will never suit you at court."

Another warning. He'd never belong in her world.

After a few minutes, Breena's breathing deepened, and he knew she'd soon be entering her dream. And then his.

Chapter 10

Breena waited before the two doors.

The plain door stood in front of her, no longer forbidden. It was even slightly ajar. For a moment she was tempted. Only pleasure awaited her on the other side.

Reluctantly she tore her gaze away and over to the ornate frame. With its jewels and promises of wealth, this would be the door most often chosen. But she knew what awaited her once she crossed the threshold. Death and destruction.

She made herself reach for the handle, turn and walk through.

This dream didn't have the usual haze, every deathly image and sound and smell was clear and stark. The zipping wisp of a razor blade caught her attention. Made her shake. She remembered. The hideous spiderlike creature that only blood magic could create. Breena swallowed back the nausea, forced herself to relearn every detail her mind had earlier wanted to reject. She looked to the stairs and saw herself there, as she was, the night of the attack. She was dressed in the beautiful gown she'd woken up wearing in Ursa. It was perfect, no longer ripped and shredded. The Breena on the stairs tried to be brave and show no fear, but each new terror, all the horror she saw before her, left its scar.

Then she saw him. A sight so frightening, so grotesque, she was almost pulled out of her dream. The Blood Sorcerer. The man responsible for it all. He was speaking to her parents, taunting them. They lay near death, their blood fueling his strength. She saw them touch hands, and she knew before she felt the zap of energy that they'd sent her away. With their combined magic, they'd planted the commands that rang in her mind more like a curse: survive and avenge. The force of her father's will and the power of her mother's magic overcame the Breena on the floor and she disappeared.

And Breena was now in Osborn's dreams.

He was waiting for her, his features no longer obscured by the dreamhaze. His firm lips, long brown hair and dark eyes familiar. She ran to him, and he caught her in his strong arms, spinning her in the air, and then allowing her to slide down the firmness of his body. She had to touch him now. Wanted to chase away the dream from behind the other door in her mind…just for a few moments.

Before, Osborn had been the aggressor. But she wasn't the same Breena that had crept into his dreams in the past. She slid her fingers into the hair at the back of his neck and pulled his lips to hers. Breena parted her lips and sank her tongue into his mouth.

Osborn groaned, holding her tight against him, meeting her forceful kiss with a growing need of his own.

"It's been so long since we've been like this," she said against his mouth.

"Too long," he echoed.

"Your choice."

"I'm an idiot," he said, and lowered his lips to hers once more. The kiss they shared was raw and passionate and filled with everything they'd denied themselves away from this dreamworld.

Breena tugged the shirt from his pants and slid her hands to his bare flesh. He sucked in a breath when her fingers trailed over his stomach. Her hands grew restless, caressing and seeking every part of him. When her palm cupped his cock, he went completely still.

"Does that feel good?" she asked.

He could only nod.

"I want to make you feel amazing. The way you made me feel by the lake," she told him as she reached for the drawstring of his pants.

Osborn stilled her hands. "No, I want to pleasure you."

"Let me," she urged. "I need this. I need to give right now." His pants loosened and she pushed them down the strength of his legs, the hair of his thighs tickling her palms. His erection sprang forward and she reached for him. He shuddered when she wrapped her fingers around his shaft. She circled the head of him with her thumb.

"Does that feel good?" she asked, loving that she already knew.

"Yes." His voice was a tight groan, and Breena felt the same kind of thrilling power that only a surge of her magic could give her.

"But it will feel better with my mouth."

His eyes flew open. The ache and the yearning for what she could do to his body was stamped on his every feature.

With a gentle push, she sent his back against a tree trunk in their dream clearing, then she sank to her knees in front of him. "Tell me if I'm doing this wrong."

"You won't."

She smiled against the soft skin of his shaft.

Kissed the tip. His legs trembled for a moment, and then he locked his knees.

Breena's hand shifted when he moved, and he grew harder between her fingers. She glided her hand up and down his rod, then found a steady rhythm, bringing the tip of him back into her mouth.

She circled him with her tongue the way he'd circled her. His harsh breath told her that no, she wasn't doing this wrong.

Breena had never seen a man so powerful, so strong, as her warrior, but he was like melted wax before her. It was exhilarating. She worked her mouth faster, and Osborn threaded his fingers through her hair, pushing himself deeper past her lips.

"Breena…"

His voice was like a strangled cry, and she quickened her pace. "Breena, you've got to—"

She awoke suddenly in her new bed.

Osborn sat on the edge of the mattress, his feet on the floor. He cradled his head in his hands, his breaths rough and uneven.

She brushed his shoulder. "Osborn?"

He flinched from her touch. Shot up from the bed like she'd zapped him with her anger-charged energy.

"Did I do something wrong?"

He shook his head, but he still wouldn't glance

her way. Bracing his hands along the trim wood of the door, Osborn kept his back to her. "We can't do that again." Then he pried open the door and left her alone.

Breena pulled the covers tight under her neck and crawled into a ball. Sleep took a long time to overcome her, but when it did her dreams bordered on nightmare.

Later that morning she found Bernt and Osborn building a new bed. "Are we going to practice?" she asked.

"Tomorrow," Osborn grunted at her, not bothering to look up.

Bernt flashed her a look that said something like "Save me" and she nodded. The frame they worked on appeared sturdy and solid. Unlike the chair in the kitchen from…just a few days ago? It felt like a life's time away.

"You do good work," she told them both.

"After about thirty tries," Bernt mumbled.

"Shut it," Osborn shot at his younger brother.

"I'd rather be practicing, too. We're not meant to be woodworkers."

"You are now."

"If you want to take a break, I wouldn't mind scabbard practice," she suggested, trying to defuse the situation, although she looked forward to scabbard practice just a little above balance work. Which was none at all.

"Breena, go away," Osborn said, his teeth gritted.

He'd never spoken so rudely to her before. Prickly, she could tolerate, but not this.

"Bernt, if you'd please excuse us. I'd like to talk with your brother in private."

Bernt dropped his hammer to the ground as if it were on fire.

"Come back here," Osborn called after his brother, but Bernt pretended not to hear. Good boy.

"One day you're going to push them away for good. Bernt and Torben look up to you. They want your approval. Why they still want that from you, who knows? Especially since you're always such a grouch to them, but they do."

Osborn's mood soured more, and his frown deepened.

"Would it hurt you to give them a smile? To say something more than just orders?" She rounded on this fuming man of hers. "Why are you so angry?"

Osborn stalked toward her, grabbed her hand and pushed it down between his legs. "This is why. Because all I can think of is shoving my cock into your mouth. Driving it into your body. Me on top. You on top. You on all fours like the beasts in the woods." He dropped her hand. "Don't be alone with me. Again."

The warning had returned.

"Be ready to work after lunch," he tossed at her

as his long strides took him into the privacy of the woods.

Breena began to tremble. All those things, every word that she knew Osborn meant to sound as a threat…she desired them, too.

Osborn hadn't been exaggerating when he'd told her to be prepared to work. Sweat ran down her temples and covered her back. He sparred with her, parrying and thrusting his sword. Expecting her to block his blade.

"You just died right then," he told her as his stick touched her shoulder. "Again."

She raised her stick, holding it in the position he'd taught her, but he powered through her defenses, his mock blade at her neck. "You're dead."

Breena shoved him away and whacked him across the legs with her stick. Then stopped and held her stick at a point just above his heart. "One plunge and you'd have taken your last breath."

"True, if you'd awoken from the dead. But it was a good surprise attack. You need more."

They bouted again and again with Breena losing every battle. "How do you expect to render justice with skills like this?" His voice was almost a taunt. He was trying to make her give up.

"My opponents won't all be Ursan warriors with a thorn in their side."

"Oh, it's way bigger than a thorn," he told her crudely.

She shoved him away. "Cool off, Osborn. Your temper is your own problem. Stop making this all my fault."

Osborn dropped his stick. "Practice is over."

"Good," she called after him. Wishing she had something more cutting to say at her disposal. Breena wiped a tear from her cheek. Who knew she could cry out of sheer irritation? She marched back to the cabin, grabbed the soap he'd given her, hating the scent as she bathed. Breena quickly dressed, needing to get as far away from the cottage and its inhabitants as fast as she could.

Torben had showed her a path that led to the bushes where they gathered ripe berries. That sounded just as good as any place. Besides the bushes, she discovered several patches of wildflowers, and she reached down to pluck a petal from one, rubbing it between her fingers and releasing the sweet scent.

How long she waited there among the flowers she didn't know, but she stiffened when she heard the footsteps she now recognized as Osborn's. He rounded a tree, his hair still wet. Probably from a soaking in the lake. Her cheeks heated at the memory of what they'd last shared at the lake, and she faced the other way.

He crouched beside her, stretching his legs out in front of him. "I've never been in a situation such as this," he told her after several moments of silence.

She expected this was Osborn's attempt at an apology, and her anger dissipated. Breena had been instructed how to behave on every conceivable social situation. But her mother had definitely missed this one.

Osborn slid something big toward her, and she glanced his way. It was one of those mysterious packages he'd brought home with him after his trip into the village. "I, uh, got this for you."

She loved gifts, and as surprising and perfect as Osborn's first present to her was, Breena couldn't wait to see what was inside this one. She pulled the end of the twine and smoothed the protective material away to reveal fine green fabric.

"It's a cloak," he told her. "The color reminded me of your eyes."

Her throat tightened. Courtiers had said charming things to her over the years, but Osborn's compliment was the most perfect. Because she knew it originated from his heart. Tears filled her eyes, and she blinked them back. How could one man send her emotions and the reason for her tears careening from one extreme to another? And so quickly?

Breena spread the cloak around her. The fashions she wore at home in Elden were much more elaborate, with tiny embroidered flowers and crystals and other small gems sewn right into the designs. But this was far more beautiful to her than anything she'd ever worn in the past. "I love it," she told him.

"There's a matching gown."

Breena reached for it, her fingers finding something round and hard instead. She plucked it out of the package to see a golden arm cuff in the shape of a snake. What an unusual adornment for jewelry. She'd never seen such a thing. Was this an Ursan custom?

"It reminded me of your first fight. How you defeated those snakelike scouts, and saved my life."

Now it made sense. Breena slid the armband into place above her elbow. "I will never take this off," she vowed to him. Just like her timepiece.

Possession quickly flowed into his brown eyes.

"Thank you," she told him as she stood. Breena clutched the gown to her chest, twirling around with the fabric. "I will wear this gown the day I return home, Osborn. The day our house is restored, and my brother Nicolai is crowned king of Elden. That's how much your gift means to me."

"Elden?" he asked, the color draining from his face. All traces of possession faded from his eyes. His gaze narrowed, and his shoulders tensed. "Did you say Elden?"

Breena nodded slowly. "That's my home. My father is—" she swallowed "—*was* king."

Osborn sprung to his feet. Away from her.

Something icy inched down her back, and she hugged the gown closer to her chest. Needing protection. Osborn no longer gazed upon her with desire and possession in his eyes, as the man she was growing to love. No, now he looked at her with something close to hate in his eyes.

"It all makes sense now," he threw at her. His words biting and hard.

"What does?" she asked, marveling at the newest change.

"I should have known when Hagan told me of Elden's fall so close to your arrival. He'd even mentioned the missing heirs. You. That is why you never told me where you were from. Elden. You knew what your people had done to mine."

"What are you talking about?"

Osborn made a scoffing sound. "Oh, you might have a problem with your memory, Breena, but not me. I remember everything. Your father chose the time of his attack well. I'll give him that. The Bärenjagd, when the warriors journeyed to our sacred bear lands. Our village was defenseless. It's a time of truce," he shouted, his voice anguished.

Breena didn't know what to say, what to do. She sucked in her bottom lip, hoping he'd continue with his story. To release all that anger before she responded to him.

"Elden was our ally. Your father saw to that," he accused. "We arrived to a massacre. And an ambush. I killed as many of your people as I could. Enjoyed watching your dead sizzle in the sunlight when it came. I taught you to fight. I brought you into my home, I shared—" He cut off his own words. "All this time you knew. You encouraged me to share my stories of the people your family killed." He stalked toward her. "Your lies won't protect you now."

Breena shook her head, backing away from him. "That's not it at all. Something inside me said not to mention Elden, some instinct." The evasion sounded terrible even to her. "But I swear, Osborn, it's not because of that. My father is an honorable king. He's a diplomat, not a fighter."

Osborn made a brutal sound. "Tell that to my mother. To my dead sister. I swore vengeance on you. On all of Elden. And I kept my hands off of you. Thinking you were something more than… Elden."

The way he said her homeland packed a punch of bitterness and venom. His hands fisted at his sides, and he lunged at her.

Breena stumbled backward, her feet catching in the folds of fabric of her gown. She landed against a tree; the rough bark poked into her shoulder blades. She could go no farther. The man had taught her many techniques when in battle with an opponent bigger and larger than herself. He probably never expected her to use any of those on him. Breena cupped his cheek. Distracting him. "Osborn…"

He paused. For one crucial moment.

"I'm sorry," she told him at the same instant she kneed him between the legs. *Hard.*

Osborn groaned and doubled over, gripping his stomach. Breena took the opportunity to push him to the ground, grabbing from her boot the knife he'd instructed her to keep hidden. She straddled him, pushing her nose to his. "I could be running away at this moment. Your instructions were to not stick around, remember?"

His eyes blazed with something past hate.

Breena lifted the blade to the beating pulse in his neck. "I could also cut you right now. See? You did manage to teach me quite a bit."

His lips thinned. She felt his skin chill and watched as his pupils began to narrow and focus. She'd triggered his berserkergang. But she wasn't scared. Breena had just spent her last moment of fear. She'd die before she felt frightened again.

And that fearsome thing inside him would not hurt her. She *knew* it.

The harshness of their breathing blanketed around them. The sun overhead created gruesome knife-wielding shadows. "My people did not attack yours."

Some of his wrath cooled. "I can see that you believe it."

It was a beginning. "You said the attackers burned in the sun?"

"Those that didn't flee. Cold-skinned cowards."

"Elden's vamps can walk in the sun. My brother Nicolai is as warm-blooded as you and me. My father was arranging an advantageous marriage to secure Elden's future. *That's* how he did things. Not through battle."

Osborn squeezed his eyes tight. She knew he was fighting her, fighting what he'd held to be true.

"They wore Elden's colors."

"It must have been a tactical move in case there were any survivors."

She watched his swallow. Emotion warred in his eyes. "Clever, because I planned my own vengeance against your people."

And with his berserker power, he would have taken the lives of a lot of her people. Although it would have been a much more merciful death than that from the Blood Sorcerer.

"I wonder if it's the same enemy. But to wait all these years…it seems unlikely."

She wanted to tell Osborn what she'd discovered in her dream. That the Blood Sorcerer killed her parents. But now this was all about Osborn.

"I'm going to drop this knife. Toss it out of the way."

That was the plan she had, nothing much more than that. Breena rolled off his big frame.

He trapped her hands before she could scramble completely out of his reach. "You know I could have overpowered you at any time."

She'd guessed it. "But you didn't."

He dropped her hands, and leaned against the tree. She watched as he scrubbed his hand along the back of his neck. "No, I didn't."

"Why not?"

His brown eyes met hers. "Because I wanted to believe you. Because I want…I want so many things since I found you in my bed."

Her stomach dipped, and her heart began to race. Many times she imagined the lover of her future. A man with courtly manners. A man who'd kiss the back of her hand. A man who'd ask for the honor of dancing with her.

Never had she imagined the man she'd want by her side to be conflicted, guilt-ravaged and so, so fallible. And yet perfect.

As a princess, Breena had two jobs, stay a virgin and marry well.

She was about to fail at one of her princessly duties.

Chapter 11

Osborn flinched when she stroked his arm. His hand instantly grasped hers, stilling her fingers.

She gave him an encouraging smile. "Let me." And his hand fell away. Breena traced the arch of his eyebrow. Ran her fingers down the length of his nose. His lips. The stubble covering his cheek. The muscles bunched below her fingertips. His strong body trembled for the briefest of moments.

"Let me love you," she urged.

The man before her tensed. Every muscle, every force of his body, tightened like her words were a physical blow to him. His eyes closed and his fists clenched at his sides. Who was he fighting now? Her or himself?

Then his lids lifted, and his gaze bore into hers. She saw all the hurt and anger he'd suffered since the attack on his home. He allowed her to see it.

"I want to love you tonight," she whispered against his neck, and she felt him shiver.

But he didn't push her away.

Her heart lifted in relief and she placed tiny little kisses on his neck, the line of his jaw and finally to his lips. Breena tugged his lower lip into her mouth with her teeth. Sucked on it until he moaned.

"Take me to your lake," she invited him. Without waiting for an answer, she tugged his hand to her mouth, kissed his palm, then drew him to his feet. They walked the short distance to the place that would always be so special to her.

After removing her boots, careful to tuck her knife inside them, she turned to him. With the water at her back, she lifted her shirt and raised it above her head, drawing the woolen fabric against her skin in sensual slowness.

"You said you hated me in boy's clothes."

"Glad they're off of you."

Her nipples puckered before his heated gaze. Osborn's brown eyes turned almost black in the dying light.

Breena walked to him slowly, loosening the pants and kicking them out of the way. He was reaching for his own shirt, but she stopped his hands of further movement. “Let me take care of you tonight.”

He swallowed. Hard. She lifted his shirt up and over his head. His pants stretched tight against his growing cock.

“These can’t be too comfortable,” she told him with a click of her tongue.

“Growing more uncomfortable by the moment,” he told her.

She smiled at this amazing man before her, feeling happy and desirable and very, very wanted. Hooking her thumbs around the material, she drew his pants down those defined legs of his, finely muscled and strong.

Osborn was magnificent. His body was honed, and crisscrossed by scars, some small, some brutal looking. She traced a jagged one beneath his collarbone. The one on his face was new, and from the night they’d first met when they battled the creature of blood magic.

Breena ran her fingers along his fine features, his jaw, his eyebrows. He gripped her hands in his, lowering his head. A breath separated their lips, and she raised on tiptoe to kiss him. He clutched her in his arms with a groan. Osborn’s kiss was a burning, searing thing, filled with pain, hope and so much passion.

His hands turned bold, palming her breast, caressing her hip, taking a lazy path down the sensitive skin of her spine. Goose bumps formed along her arms and her nipples tightened against the rough-haired strength of his chest. She couldn't get enough of touching him. Just running her hands over the roped muscles of his arms shot little thrills through her body.

"Look at me," he urged, his voice raw with passion.

Her lids drifted open as his questing fingers rounded her hips and cupped her bottom. With a jerk, he brought her flush against his naked skin. The hardness of his erection left no doubt how much he wanted her, and her knees weakened.

Osborn scooped her up into his arms, and stalked to the soft sandy bank of the lake.

"I was supposed to be taking care of you," she told him with a laugh.

"Next time," he promised, his voice rough and filled with need.

"Yes." She nodded. Now and quickly. She looped her arms around his neck and drew his head down to hers once more. His lips parted hers, and his tongue surged inside her mouth. Their kiss was urgent and hurried.

He drew her down with him; the gentle lap of water at their feet was warm and sensual. Osborn stretched alongside her, his mouth and hands seeking her breasts. His lips teased and tormented her nipple until he finally drew her into the warmth of his mouth. Breena arched to meet him, her body aching and slick for the joining of their bodies. She'd been ready for this man a lifetime. Across her dreams to his.

"We have to take this slow, Breena. This will be your first time, and I don't want to hurt you."

"Then touch me." She ached for his hands in her most secret of places.

"Here?" he asked, skimming the skin of her rib cage.

"Lower."

Now his hand smoothed over her belly. "What about here?"

"Lower," she urged.

His fingers slid easily along the wetness between her legs.

"Yes." Her voice was a moan. A wave of sensation flooded her at his caress.

"Touching is good, but I'd rather taste." Osborn hooked one of her legs over his shoulder, then kissed where her very awareness seemed centered.

Osborn circled his tongue, ramping up her pleasure. She felt the gentle probe of his finger. He slid inside her, and her inner muscles clamped.

"This is going to be so good," he told her, then proved it by laving her with his tongue.

A second finger joined the first, and he gave a tiny thrust that left her aching and needing release. Her whole body began to surge and tremble.

"Don't make me wait anymore, Osborn."

A line formed between his brows. "I don't want to hurt you. I'd do anything not to cause you pain."

"I don't care. I need you. Need you inside me. Now."

He moved between her legs, his cock so long and thick she almost rethought her readiness. He positioned himself where his fingers had been.

"Watch," he told her. "See your body welcoming mine."

With gentle pressure, he thrust inside her, found the barrier of her virginity and broke through.

There was pain, but there was so much more. The weight of him on her body. The gentle kiss he placed on her temple. The pleasure shaping his beautiful face. And then the pain was gone. Replaced by a blissful frenzy. The fullness of him. The length of him inside her. Osborn began to move his hips and her tender body grew used to the motion.

"Harder?" he asked.

Breena didn't know if harder was what she wanted but she was willing to give it a try. "Yes," she whispered.

Osborn complied. Yes, harder was definitely what she wanted. He thrust again and again, going faster, the sensations growing more intense. Breena raised her hips to meet his hips. Needing more of him. She'd experienced pleasure with him once before. She craved that now. Her thirst for the thrill building and building.

"Wrap your legs behind my back," he instructed.

The change brought the core of her need hard up against his thrusts. Osborn licked below her ear. Squeezed her breast. He was everywhere. Over her. In her. She breathed him inside her with each breath she took.

"You feel so good, Breena."

The raw pleasure in his words sent her over the edge. She gasped. "Osborn, I'm—"

"Yes, Breena, yes," and he surged within her.

A current of sensation shimmered through her body, and she squeezed the hard length of him. With a groan, his back stiffened and he poured himself into her.

Spent, he slumped against her, balancing the bulk of his weight on his arms. They lay there together, unable to move. Then Osborn rolled to his back, taking her with him, and cradled her head against his chest.

Breena couldn't imagine sharing something so intimate with anyone but Osborn. When Elden was restored, she'd refuse any match Nicolai would make on her behalf. She wanted no one but Osborn. His arms holding her tight. His lips on hers. His body giving her pleasure.

She trailed her fingertip along the warm skin

of his chest. "Does your berserker ever come out when…you know."

Osborn laughed, and she closed her eyes in pleasure. *She* had done this to him. Made him happy. Lifted him from the agony he'd consigned himself to. Breena had never truly understood or appreciated the gift that was her magic.

"Give me a few minutes and we can try."

All that force and strength and power, it was a little daunting. "How did you become berserker?"

Osborn twined his fingers with hers. "Our ancestors tell us man and bear were once one *bermannen*. *Bermannen* and his mate were clever, too clever for the gods' liking. They captured the secrets of lightning and made fire. They stole the key to the clouds and could control the weather. *Bermannen* and his mate even grew wise enough to discover the mysteries of the soil to grow their own food. The two needed nothing from the gods."

Breena propped herself up on her elbow to gaze down at Osborn. "What happened?" She knew many tales, but none that involved the Ursan deities.

"The gods grew jealous, so they separated the two. All the strength and power went to bear, while wisdom went to man. *Mannen* and *ber* cried to be united. Then grew angry. The berserker rage comes from our need to be as one, and it cannot ever fully be. Feeling pity, the gods gave man the gift of his use of fire and knowledge of the land. Bear received strength, and sacred lands where they are free to roam."

"You did know a story."

"*Ber* and *mannen* were broken, but they were still clever and discovered a way to defeat the gods and their interference."

"How?"

"Through death the two spirits merge. Bear and man battle, but only one can win."

"You fought a bear to become berserker?"

Osborn pointed to the scar crossing his body. Breena gasped, then traced the path of the scar. Leaned down to kiss it.

"I am one with *ber,* but only through his honorable death. The berserkergang is always there, but it's the pelt that merges us, makes me what you saw in the alley, and why I couldn't kill the scout here at the lake."

"You were naked. And that pelt you wear was the bear's. That's so sad."

Osborn raised a brow. "Are you wishing the bear had won? Often they do."

She shook her head quickly.

"Man can merge with bear, or bear can join with man. It is our way." Osborn lifted her hand from his chest. "I love your tender heart."

Her heart slammed into her ribs. Love. He loved her heart. It was a start.

He kissed each one of her fingers. Sucking on the last.

"Yesterday when you were bathing, I heard you gasp. Were you thinking of me, Breena? Were you touching yourself and thinking of me?"

She swallowed the lump that formed in her throat and willed herself not to blush. Breena could only nod.

A slow satisfied smile spread across his face. "I'd like to watch."

His request sounded so outrageous, she sputtered.

"Feel how the idea of it gets me." Osborn took her hand, and placed it on the hard length of his cock.

Moisture gathered between her legs. "You really want to see that?"

"Gods, yes. Here—" he tweaked her nipple "—and here." His fingers delved into her woman's heat. "Sit up."

Breena braced herself off the ground, and Osborn reached for her hips.

"Straddle me."

Me on top. You on top. You on all fours like the beasts in the woods.

Those words of his had hollowed her. Intrigued her. Made her burn.

Breena lifted herself up onto him, and he grew in length.

"Put me inside."

There was that weak feeling again. Breena reached for his cock, smooth and hard. She gripped him gently and he groaned. "I wanted you that day as I was bathing," she told him. "Wanted it to be you touching me."

"Me, too," he told her, his body shaking with the need to plunge.

"Watch," she urged. Now it was her turn to give the orders. Breena positioned the tip of him where their bodies met and sank down his length. Filling her. She shivered with the exquisite perfect sensation of their joined bodies.

Osborn's eyes closed on a deep moan, his hands lifted to cup her breasts.

Her breasts heated at his touch, her nipples tightened. She lifted herself high, until he almost left her body, then she slammed back down again. His hips bucked, and he gripped her waist, trying to take control.

"Touch yourself. Like that day," he told her, his voice raspy and tight. His eyes dark.

Her whole body trembled at his request. Bracing herself on Osborn's broad shoulders, Breena sat back on her heels, her fingers lowering. She circled her nipples, feeling them pucker even more. Slowly, she let her fingers drift down. Osborn's heated gaze followed the slow, sensuous path she took. Down over her rib cage, past her stomach, until she met the curls that hid where they joined.

She gasped at the first light touch between her legs.

"Yes," her lover encouraged, and thrust.

She rubbed herself more forcefully, feeling the crest surge. Her inner muscles clamped down hard on his length. Osborn gripped her hips, keeping her in place as he thrust. Breena's fingers grew more frantic.

Her nipples tightened, every muscle in her body stretched. Reached for him and what he could give her.

"Harder," she demanded.

He gripped her tighter, his every movement bringing him deeper inside her body. With a gasp, he drove her over the edge. Crest after crest of sensation poured through Breena. His name came from her lips in a moan.

She felt Osborn's chest strain and his fingers dig into her skin. In one quick movement, he rolled her onto her back. Hooking her legs behind his back she drew him closer to her still. Reveled in the feel of his weight over her, his strength pinning her to the ground.

"Yes. Like that," she encouraged.

He surged inside her, his thrusts deeper. Harder. Every muscle of his body stiffened as his climax hit, and triggered something deep inside her.

Tingles of another peak flared, and she held him to her as hard as she could.

Breena returned to herself slowly. The lapping of the lake, the wind in the trees, the call of a distant bird and the welcome weight of the large, loving man above her. Her heartbeat slowed and she could finally draw in breath without sounding like she'd just sparred with Osborn on the practice field.

Osborn rolled onto his back, taking her with him and tucking her against his side. He kissed the top of her head.

"I love you," she whispered to him. Then fell asleep.

Osborn squeezed his eyes tight. He hadn't known how much he needed those words until she'd uttered them so delightfully in her sleep. He hugged her tight. She deserved a better man than he was. Someone more honorable. Someone who could give her the same words.

She deserved more, but that didn't mean he wouldn't fight or kill to keep her at his side. Osborn wasn't an idiot.

One day merged into another far too quickly. By day Osborn would continue with Breena's and his brothers' training. Her magic was growing stronger, and she could control small bursts without needing emotion as her medium. The nights were his and Breena's. Most evenings he joined her in the tiny sleeping room. Other nights they spent near the lake and under the stars…and he thought about full moons.

Bernt and Torben were growing to be fine, strong men, despite him. He'd introduced the tradition of ending each evening in front of a large fire, as his people had when he was a boy. There he told his brothers of the *bermannen* and his mate and their angering of the gods.

He shared the traditions of their parents, how they sealed their life together, and how their father had trained and prepared Osborn for his Bärenjagd.

The unsettled anger within Bernt lessened each day.

The three of them had lived on the sacred bear land all these years, with only Osborn's vow to protect this place. No bear had stalked Bernt to become *bermannen*. To become berserker. And yet Bernt had to be the age for his Bärenjagd. Well past. And yet he grew powerful.

Had Osborn changed the destinies of both *ber* and man when he came here to live? Once when sparring, Osborn thought he'd wounded his younger brother with his blade, but there wasn't even a scratch. Berserkers couldn't be harmed by steel. Dare he test Bernt with the only substances that could defeat a berserker? Weapons made of tree and fire. Tree, because it grew from the ground, and fire, because it was the gift to man by the gods. Those jealous deities must have found it ironic that their gifts could also bring about death.

Osborn imagined a life for his brothers with no Bärenjagd. Strength and honor without the struggle and blood? But those thoughts would have to wait for another time…after. But after what, he couldn't say.

Later that evening he followed the sound of his brothers' laughter. He found them around the fire, laughing with Breena. "What's so funny?" he asked.

"Breena was just about to make good on her threat of teaching Bernt to dance."

"That's not a threat," she told them with mock sternness. "Dancing is an important life skill."

"Mother liked to dance," Osborn said.

Bernt looked up sharply, his expression eager. Right now he was more boy than man, hungry to hear more.

Osborn had cheated them. Took away from them the comfort of their memories and the stories he could tell of them because he was selfish. All because *he* didn't want to remember. *He* didn't want the pain. It wasn't his brothers' guilt. It wasn't their shame. Torben and Bernt should be able to love a mother and father.

"When did she dance?" Torben asked, his

voice quiet, as if he were almost afraid he'd anger Osborn and this moment would vanish.

"During the first night of the full moon, we'd gather in the center of our village. The elders would light a large bonfire, and we'd eat, and sing and dance. You liked to chase each other around the fire, which always make mother worry."

A smile spread across Bernt's face. "I remember."

"Did you dance?" Torben asked Osborn.

He shook his head. He would have been dancing. The year after his Bärenjagd. "I never learned."

"Breena should teach you."

"Oh, I doubt your brother would want to learn anything like that," she said, clearly hoping to discourage any further attempts. For his sake? Or hers?

Now he smiled openly. That seemed very much like a challenge, and he never backed away from a dare. He brushed his palms along his thighs and stood, extending his hand toward her.

"It's time I learned."

Breena felt the muscles of her face fall in astonishment. Osborn could have said a lot of things at the moment, but she never would have guessed he'd ask her to dance. Or want a lesson. He'd never stop surprising her.

"Show me how they dance where you come from, Breena."

His voice was pure invitation, and she couldn't resist. She placed her hand in his, and allowed him to direct her to a clearing while his younger brothers poked each other in the ribs. He made to gather her in his arms, which finally snapped her to the task at hand. She'd taken his barking instruction, his incessant demands she work harder and performed the maneuvers again and again. Now it was her turn to issue a few commands of her own.

"A gentleman doesn't just grab a lady and jostle her about."

"There's something obvious I could point out here," he told her.

Was that actually humor lacing his words? She chose to ignore it and flashed him her best imitation of Osborn's I'm-training-you-so-pay-very-close-attention expression.

"You stand beside me, and only our shoulders touch." She'd better amend that to side. None of her previous partners had ever towered quite as tall as Osborn. Breena twirled her finger in her hair. "And we face opposite directions."

Osborn dropped his arms from around her shoulders and rotated so that he aligned himself against her side. She was sure this particular dance was designed so that young men and ladies would remain respectable and refined, and Breena had never thought of it as anything untoward. But his hip brushed against hers in a way that was anything but harmless and breathed in his heat and the earthy scent of him.

"Now what?" he prompted.

She glanced up to see his dark gaze boring into hers. "You raise your arm, and I drape my hand over it."

He followed her direction and Breena realized that sometime in the last few minutes she'd lost the upper hand. And she didn't like it. She cleared her throat. "It's important to remember that once on the dance floor, the woman always leads."

The biggest lie she'd ever told, but she doubted Osborn would ever know. Besides, it was fun to tell this warrior what to do. "This particular dance has very precise movements timed to the music. First we circle to my right. Then to my left."

Osborn moved slowly, his gaze never leaving her face.

"Next you drop your hand to my waist, and we circle again."

His hand slid slowly, intimately down her body. She adored dancing. It was her favorite thing to do at Elden.

Not anymore.

"Go to bed, boys," Osborn ordered.

If the days passed too quickly, the nights flew. Each morning he woke up with a sense of foreboding. Something sinister loomed in the distance. He intensified the level of Breena's workout. She'd made herself into an excellent swordswoman, but he feared this strong, brave woman would never have the brute strength to defeat soldier after soldier. They had to focus on her defenses.

Osborn raised his weapon. "Distract me," he ordered.

"Have you ever made love with your pelt on?" she asked.

Osborn nearly dropped his sword, and the hilt fumbled in his palm.

Breena couldn't help but smile, and took the opportunity to advance. But he countered her thrust.

"No," he told her, his bottom lip growing more sensual.

"Oh." The idea of it had intrigued her ever since he'd explained it was only in his pelt that he was fully berserker. She'd hoped he might know how the *ber* spirit inside him reacted in passion.

He was so strong and powerful and solely focused when enraged. How would it feel to have all that strength and force and attention centered on her?

She knew man nor berserker would ever harm her, but would making love add an edge of danger?

Soon she'd have to leave this cottage and face the threat in her realm. Despite Osborn's training and the growing strength of her magical powers, she had to face the reality that she might not live. She might die the last heir of Elden. Breena had a lifetime's worth of experience to cram into only a short time. And making love to her man in full berserker frenzy was something she wanted to experience.

"Osborn?" she asked as she parried.

"Yes?"

"Did you notice I'm alone with you?"

He lowered his weapon, and rammed it home in its scabbard. Clearly there'd be no more training this afternoon. "I seem to remember warning you about being alone with me."

"And here I am, disregarding your warnings. Do you remember what you promised? I mean, threatened?"

He shook his head, but his eyes grew narrow and the air around them chilled.

"You on top. Me on top. You taking me on all fours like a beast."

"I remember now." His words turned heavy with desire.

Breena lifted the pack that was never out of reach and tossed it to him. "I'm going to run now."

She dropped her sword to the ground, and took off, hoping the animal spirit in him would not be able to resist a chase. Breena didn't stand in the practice clearing long enough to find out. She raced along the path with a laugh, removing her shirt as she ran. Her pants were a little more difficult to take off, but soon she managed to be running only in her light undergarments.

The air around her chilled, despite the sun's rays over her head. *He was berserker.* Excitement and the thrill of the danger sent her faster down the path. Behind her the leaves of the trees rustled, announcing he wasn't too far away.

"Breena," he called, his voice tight and otherworldly. Not completely human. She'd never heard him speak in full berserker rage.

A thick arm curved around her waist and her feet no longer raced along the path. Osborn shoved her against the trunk of a large tree, the bark pressing into her breasts. His hands sought the tiny bows at her hips and ripped. The cloth hiding her woman's places fell to the ground and his fingers slipped between her legs.

He bucked up against her when he felt her wetness, and his cock nestled against her backside. He nipped at her shoulder with his teeth. His love play was rougher and tinged with danger. More wet heat flooded between her legs. He gripped her breasts; they were hard and needed his touch. He pinched at her nipples and she shivered all the way down to her toes.

"Are you mine, Breena?" he asked, his voice was ragged and uneven.

"Yes." *Always.*

"Lift your leg."

She raised her knee, the bark rubbing against her inner thigh. He probed her with the tip of his cock, then sank inside her with a groan. "Mine," he said, squeezing her breast. He thrust and her whole body shook, the length of him so hard and thick with this new angle. His pelt shrouded them both. Osborn rocked inside her, the waves and crests of Breena's desire building and building. Her moans echoed throughout the trees. She was so close….

Osborn pulled out of her heat, his breath harsh behind her.

"On the ground. On your knees," he bit out, the words difficult to get out over his hunger.

She turned and leaned against the bark and stared at her berserker. His eyes were nearly black. Strain and tension molded his face. His hands fisted at his sides and his muscles were coiled, ready for battle. Osborn was beautiful in his rage, a fearsome yet awesome sight. His cock stretched straight from his body.

Breena lowered to the ground. Osborn dropped to his knees behind her, smoothed his hand along her back and kissed her shoulder. His fingers found the place where her pleasure centered and he caressed it. Her senses blazed. She needed him inside her.

"Osborn. *Now.*"

With an aching groan he gripped her hips and brought her to his body. She felt the heat of his probing erection, and then he thrust inside. Breena began to shiver and quake at the sensation. Osborn moved inside her, in and out, and once more she was moaning in pleasure.

"More," she urged. She wanted every part of her lover. Needed her warrior.

He pushed his hips more forcefully and finally she slipped over the edge of her desire. Her muscles clamped around his length and she could do nothing but feel. Around her the air swirled, and with a harsh groan, his body was racked by his climax.

Osborn collapsed on the ground, nearly too worn out to tuck her into his side. After a few moments, he kissed the top of her head. "I never lose control like that. I didn't hur—"

Breena lifted up on her arm and placed a finger across his lips. "You didn't lose control. I knew you could never hurt me."

She hugged this man tightly to her chest, her body still fluttering. Osborn had brought so much pleasure into her life. New experiences. She wouldn't be who she was right now if it weren't for him. A part inside her sobered. Was this the woman she was meant to be? If the Blood Sorcerer hadn't attacked everything would have stayed the same. She would have gone on being Princess Breena.

But the attacks did happen. Her parents were

murdered, her realm most likely destroyed, the people who looked to the royal family for protection and continuity dead or enslaved. While she found bliss in the arms of a man.

Breena was quiet the rest of the day, and he grew more worried. What if he really had hurt her, and she was trying to hide it? Why had he done it? Worn his pelt and chased after her? It was insanity.

Because she asked you.

And Osborn would do anything Breena requested of him. But not that again, he vowed. Never again. The idea of causing her harm made him hurt.

He watched her, helpless as she suffered through dinner. She had no stories to share at the campfire. By evening he was filled with guilt over his weakness. Osborn had to fix it. He followed her to her room that evening.

"You've been quiet all day," he said as he joined her in the bed. She hadn't told him to go and leave her alone, so he took that as a good sign.

"I was thinking about how happy I am."

A rush of relief almost made him shake. Osborn laced his fingers with hers. "That's a good thing."

Breena shook her head. "No, it's not. I shouldn't be happy. Not when my people are suffering. When my parents are dead."

Cold streaked through him. Not the kind that

signaled the return of his berserkergang, but from panic. It was happening. He'd feared Breena would become guilt plagued…like him. It would eat at her now that it had taken root. The blame she'd heap on herself would tear at her soul, leaving her anguished and filled with regret.

He wanted to take her into his arms, and assure her that the death of her family was not her fault. Smooth the line forming between her brows,and tell her she had nothing to feel guilty over.

But he didn't, because he knew she wouldn't believe him. Just as he didn't believe those same things about his own life.

They didn't make love that night. Instead, they lay side by side, barely touching.

He awoke the next morning with that same feeling of doom.

Osborn disentangled himself from the bedcoverings, and stared down at Breena's beautiful face. He'd never grow tired of gazing at her. Even if he were privileged enough to grow old with her, see lines fanning from her eyes, and more gray than blond strands in her silky hair. It wasn't her features that made her beautiful to him. It was her spirit. Her capacity to love, both him and his brothers, despite all that had been ripped from her life. Breena hadn't feared the berserker in him. That's when it all changed for him. She wasn't afraid of anything.

While he was filled with fear.

He'd lose her. He knew it to be true now. Osborn had probably held on to her a little too long already.

After slipping out of her bed, he quickly dressed. He could no longer put off journeying into the village and seeking news of Elden. That was what loomed in the distance. Breena's revenge and her dreams of seeing her brothers, if they were still alive, restored to the throne. It was time for her to fulfill and silence the commands—no, the curses—her parents instilled in her mind. Survive and avenge…survive *to* avenge.

The village was quiet as he crested the hill, most of its residents still asleep. All but the merchants. Osborn found the spice man unpacking his wares, and arranging the items for optimal display. The man smiled at his approach. "I told you to stock up on olive oil before my supply dried up. Now it's all gone. Elden is a fortress."

"What I need is information."

The merchant only smiled. "The cost is the same. I'm a businessman, after all."

Osborn dug in his pack, and handed over the coin.

"I'm afraid the news is not good, my friend. Can't get anything in and out of Elden now. There's talk the land is cursed by blood." The merchant shuddered. "I will not go back, not even for the fortune I'd make."

Cursed by blood. The snake scout made by blood magic. It all confirmed Breena's dream memory. The Blood Sorcerer was behind the attacks on Elden. "What of Elden's people?"

The spice man shook his head. "Of them I know even less, although with such little information, I'd suspect they were all dead."

Osborn had suspected as much, too. Breena's beloved brothers…Nicolai, Dayn and little Micah.

"There are rumors of a resistance."

Finally. Some good news.

"What?"

The merchant held up his empty palms. Clever ploy. Dropping his story at its most suspenseful.

Osborn slid more coins the spice man's way. "If I learn your talk was all lies to gain my money, you'll find yourself joining the dead of Elden."

"No, my information is solid. Those loyal to Elden's memory are gathering in an outbuilding along the border. Each day more return to gather arms and plan an attack. A fool's last stand, if you ask me."

And Breena should be there to lead her people.

Osborn had still been foolish enough to hold a small sliver of hope that Breena would stay. Hadn't realized it until that hope just died. He should have known better. In the stories she shared around the firelight at night, the princess never remained in the cottage in the woods.

On his way out of the valley, Osborn secured the provisions they'd need for their travel to Elden. To the place where her people gathered, very likely awaiting a leader. He'd learned the positions of the stars as a child, and could easily lead her home.

The walk through the tree-lined path that would lead him back to Breena did not take long. With a quick knock to her bedroom door, he stepped inside. She smiled up at him, and stretched her morning sleep away.

"I was just wondering where you'd gone." She scooted to the side and flipped back the bedcovering. "Now you can come back to bed."

He did not move.

Her welcoming smile faded. "Osborn, what is it?"

"I have news of your people."

Her beautiful green eyes widened.

"They're forming a resistance. They hope to take back the castle."

Breena squeezed her eyes tight. "Yes." Then she whirled off the bed, quickly retrieving fresh clothes. "We've got to get there as soon as possible."

"I've readied our packs."

"I must gather my things. Do they know that I'm still alive? What a foolish question. Of course not. How would they even know? I wonder who's leading them? And I'm talking so fast you can't catch up."

His lips turned up in a grin despite his souring mood. "You're excited. It's okay."

Breena gripped his elbow. "It *is* going to be okay, isn't it? I can feel it."

"Finish packing what you need. I'm going to give some instructions to my brothers."

Bernt flashed Osborn an accusatory glare when he stepped outside, blinking under the sun.

"I want to keep her," Torben told him, sounding more boy than man.

"She doesn't belong to us," he tried to explain.

Bernt shook his head. "But you could make her stay. Tell her what she wants to hear."

I love you.

Please stay.

I'm dying inside at the thought of you leaving me.

He ground his back teeth. "This is her path. We've always known that."

"What about after? She'd come back if you asked her to."

"I have no right to ask. Besides, she's a princess. Princesses belong in castles."

Bernt turned on his heel and stalked into the wilderness. There'd be no goodbyes from his younger brother.

Chapter 12

They traveled for three days. Osborn didn't want to rush their pace, despite Breena's urge to run.

"At the end of this journey there *will* be a battle, Breena. We can't afford to be worn out before the first strike," he warned.

At night they made love where they camped, their couplings sometimes fierce, sometimes savoring, but always tinged with a touch of desperation. Osborn would hold her long after she fell asleep, staring up at the stars.

"What are you doing?" she'd ask sleepily.

"Willing time to slow."

Sometime after their noon meal on the third day, he discovered the whereabouts of the outbuilding.

Breena gasped when she spotted tents dotting the area and her people milling about—families, soldiers, workers of the castle.

"My people," she whispered, filled with so much relief and love she could hardly breathe.

"There's Rolfe," she nearly shouted, and Breena rushed toward him before Osborn could stop her.

Breena charged across the field with new energy, the breeze lifting her hair and cooling her face. The people working outside stopped to stare, their jaws dropping open in shock and their eyes filling with tears. Her people crowded her, welcoming her.

"Word of my brothers? Has anyone heard anything of them?" she shouted above the din.

But the Eldens continued to rejoice that one of the heirs had been returned to them.

"Rolfe," she called.

The man turned at the sound of his name. Rolfe had once been an important member of their household, part of the security that guarded her parents. Age had crept over him since she last saw him. He looked drawn and defeated. His eyes grew larger and joy touched the edges of his face when he recognized her. Then his face drained of color.

Guilt. She knew that emotion well.

"It wasn't your fault," she rushed to assure him. "How could a small personal force defeat the Blood Sorcerer?"

"You shouldn't be here," he warned.

How silly for Rolfe to be worried about propriety right now. "Nonsense. These are my people. This is exactly where I belong."

"How'd you get here?" Rolfe's gaze searched the crowd, spotting the other newcomer, Osborn. "You—" he pointed "—get her out of here."

Osborn's hand immediately went to the hilt of his sword.

The door of the outbuilding opened, and out stepped a man, and the crowd hushed. Breena recognized him as a member of the group who'd once protected Elden's perimeters. "What's all this commotion?" he shouted. It was a loud booming voice coming from someone so gaunt.

Instantly the Eldens began to shrink away and cower.

"Why are you yelling when all they are doing is enjoying the day?" she asked, her voice stern.

"Cedric has been, uh, leading the people."

Breena suppressed a shudder. Cedric had always seemed a particularly nasty sort, but then war made strange allies, and she glanced at Osborn. He was scanning the crowd, his hand remaining on his weapon.

"Sometimes a little force is needed to quiet and keep things orderly. You understand, I'm sure."

No, she didn't understand.

"I want no more of it. These people are scared.

They've lost loved ones and fear for what's in the future. We need no more strife and anger."

Cedric's lips curled over his teeth in what she supposed was to be a smile. It looked more like a snarl.

"Thank you for all that you've accomplished, Cedric. Your deeds will not go unnoticed," she added. And warned.

Osborn stepped forward. "Tell me your resources."

Cedric stiffened, as if he was about to argue, then his gaze took in the strength and breadth of Osborn's shoulders, and the massive sword at his hip.

"Nicolai is gathering a vast force in the south."

The joy and relief of hearing that news almost made her double over. "My brother is alive?"

Cedric nodded. "Dayn, too. He's leading an army, as well. Word is the Blood Sorcerer's hold on Elden is already weakening. These will be our lands again," he said, loud enough for the entire crowd to hear.

A great cheer sounded, and Breena understood why they followed Cedric. Perhaps her first impression of him was wrong. Times of trouble could often bring out character in a person, and add inner strength. With her, it brought out a fighter.

Cedric's glance fell to Osborn. "Thank you for escorting the princess back to her homeland. You will be greatly rewarded for your troubles. Rolfe, bring me the gold we'd set aside. We feared if you'd been captured, we'd have to pay a ransom."

She glanced at Osborn, whose eyes had narrowed, his stance on alert.

"I'll have you escorted away from here in a few moments. I'm sure you can't wait to be on your way. There's a village half a day's walk to the east. I'm sure you're anxious to spend your coin."

"You're confusing Osborn for a mercenary," she told him. "He didn't bring me here for a reward."

"But you *are* a mercenary, aren't you?"

Osborn nodded slowly.

Rolfe returned with a purse heavy with gold. Cedric grabbed the bag and tossed it at Osborn, who caught it against his chest.

She glanced toward her warrior but he wouldn't meet her gaze. His stare was locked on the man who'd just called him a mercenary.

Cedric grabbed the shoulder of a passing boy. "Fetch Asher and Gavin." Cedric met Osborn's stare. "They're our two best soldiers. They'll escort you off Elden lands immediately."

"What are you talking about?" she asked. "Of course Osborn is staying."

"Are you staying, mercenary? With a princess?" His question was more of a sneer. Cedric was making Osborn sound like an opportunist. One only out for himself.

Her stomach began to tense. “Osborn?”

“She’s with her people now. Two great armies are on their way. There’s no reason for you to be here.”

Tense silence stretched between them. This was so very silly. She opened her mouth to tell—

“No. There’s no reason for me to stay.”

“What?” she asked, hurt and confused. This had to be a strategy, some kind of ruse Osborn employed to test the security.

“Here come our soldiers now,” Cedric announced, his voice betraying his delight.

“I’ll have a word in private with my mercenary,” she informed them all.

Cedric looked like he wanted to argue, but then bowed his head in acquiescence.

Osborn followed her to a tree away from Cedric and Rolfe. “What’s your plan?” she asked.

Her warrior scrubbed his hand down his face. “Walk back home. Train my brothers.”

She felt sick. “You really *are* leaving?”

Osborn angled his head around camp. “They seem to have everything in order here. Your brothers are coming.”

“And you’re just leaving me here?”

His nod was her answer.

“But…but you’re my warrior. You belong with me.”

He gripped her arms. “You’ve built me up in

your mind, made me something I'm not. You've made me into one of your fairy-tale heroes." His dark eyes burned into hers. "But I'm just a man. A man who wanted you any way he could have you."

"Like a soul mate?"

At least that sounded romantic.

But Osborn the warrior only shook his head. "I don't believe in soul mates. I don't believe in anything but pleasure and passion."

Her body began to tremble. She didn't want to look at him. "I've just been fooling myself that you care, haven't I?"

Osborn swallowed and his gaze clashed with hers. He looked like he wanted to argue with her words. *Please argue. Please tell me I'm wrong.*

"We've enjoyed each other. Now it's over."

Breena would not cry in front of this man. She would not cry over him. Ever. "Go," she told him, turning her back.

He waited a moment, and she almost turned around to grab his hand. But then she heard his boots rustle in the fallen leaves. Osborn was leaving her.

"And, mercenary…"

"Yes?"

"Don't come back."

After gulping in several large breaths, Breena turned toward Cedric and Rolfe.

"Come inside, princess," Cedric invited. "See what's been prepared for your family's return to the castle."

With a nod, she followed him into the outbuilding. Dayn had told her this had been the original keep of Elden, when their realm was new and not so vast. The ceiling only topped to a second floor, so much smaller than the high-beamed castle that was her home. Would be her home again…until she was matched with a suitable marriage prospect. Her heart tightened, knowing that it would not be Osborn at her side. In her bed.

Made of stone and wood, the walls of the outbuilding were stained black from the years of fires in the hearth. A fire now blazed once more for the people who'd sought refuge here. Over the years, this had become a storage house, filled with the casks of wines and oils produced on their lands and sold.

"I've brought you a gift," Cedric told someone in the shadows.

"Is that what all that cheering was about outside?"

Breena shuddered. Goose bumps raised on her arms and along the back of her neck. That voice induced chills. Evil. It was all she could think.

"Leyek, I present Breena, the princess of Elden."

"Alive, how delightful," the voice said, still hidden in the shadows.

Cedric was working for the Blood Sorcerer. His gaunt appearance made sense now. How the Blood Sorcerer's minions were able to break their outer walls—the area Cedric protected. Now she understood Rolfe's words when he first spotted her. *You shouldn't be here.*

The people she thought warming themselves by the fire were tied to hooks in the floor. Men and women and two small girls not much older than four, their faces frightened. Their fate was a blood draining.

"That vast army you spoke of, it's a lie, isn't it?" she asked. But she knew the answer. No one would be coming to save her or her people. The saving was all up to her.

"Your brothers are as dead as your parents," Cedric sneered, and spat on the ground. "I rule here now."

"As a minion. And to the Blood Sorcerer. The both of you."

"Take the princess," Leyek ordered, still not coming out of the shadows. Demonstrating his low opinion of Elden. "Tie her. She'll make a delicious meal for our Blood Lord."

She truly valued Osborn's insistence she practice sliding her sword from her scabbard over and over again. The only time she could make a stand would be now. It would be her one chance.

Her fingers gripped the hilt.

Why the hell was he going?

These were new times. Different and desperate times. A menace threatened their world—all the realms. It could be years or only days away, but soon they'd all face the reckoning. There may be little left after the battle. What pleasure, what *love,* anyone could grab…*he'd* grab that now with both hands. It didn't matter that she was a princess, and even if it did…he wouldn't care. Osborn would offer anything of himself she'd take. Breena was his pleasure. His love.

Those responsible for the deaths of his mother and sister and father, and the people of his village…he may never know their identity.

Something ripped inside him. A painful acknowledgment that there may never be an opportunity for him to avenge his family. That understanding hurt so fiercely, so brutally, that he almost keened over the loss of what had been his steady companion since returning from his Bärenjagd. Osborn gulped in deep breaths, forcing his heart to slow, his stomach to settle.

But there was still a chance for Breena.

Still a chance for her to free her people. To find her brothers. To do something, *anything,* to shake the ever-present need for revenge.

Why would he leave her now? He would fight alongside her. Fight to bring peace to her land or die, sword in hand at her flank.

But Osborn didn't plan on dying.

Osborn turned on his heel, ready to charge into the outbuilding where he'd left her. Ready to seal his fate to hers.

The steel clang of Breena sliding her sword from its scabbard slowed his step.

He *knew* it was Breena's sword. He'd heard that sound many, many times. Made her practice often enough until her movements were fluid and smooth. So that she'd draw her sword quickly enough to spring a surprise hit.

Why would she be drawing it now? Among her welcoming people?

Cold began to creep up his legs and spread throughout his body. He dropped everything but his sword and his pelt. His berserkergang was alert and anxious for a fight. Osborn slipped into the outbuilding through a side door. He spotted Breena as she stood in battle stance, her sword protecting her body, her eyes alert. She was magnificent.

And she was *his*.

The man who'd welcomed his princess back so heartily a few minutes ago, gave Osborn gold to leave, now raised his weapon to her.

Rage pounded in his chest. Anger flashed white-hot in front of his eyes. With the cry of his berserker rage, Osborn raised his sword and charged. In less than a heartbeat, the man's sword clanged to the floor, his body not much farther behind.

Osborn stalked in front of Breena and raised his sword. "Who dies next?" he asked.

A low whistle sounded in the back of the room. Osborn felt Breena stiffen, and knew whoever made that sound was the threat.

"Show yourself," Osborn commanded.

"Or you'll what? Kill these fine Elden citizens? Do it. You'd be saving me the effort. Although…"

The slow scrape of a chair across the floor alerted Osborn he was about to see who'd tried to harm Breena.

"I do like the idea of you getting a good look at my face—as it will be the last thing you see." A tall, thin shell of a man walked out of the shadows.

Osborn's berserker stirred again. He'd heard the rumors of what blood sorcery would do to a person. Drain them of what once made them human. First their senses, until they craved hearing only the agonized cries of others and hungered solely for the taste of near death. Then all emotion would flee from their souls—first empathy, then remorse, until finally only hostility and greed remained. Lastly, their bodies would change. The curves and planes and every range of compassionate expressions of the face vanished until finally only a walking, breathing carcass remained.

"Leyek is strong. And brutal," Breena whispered, and Osborn understood. This minion of the Blood Sorcerer might look frail, but that was an illusion. His power was indomitable, tinged with great evil.

Osborn became one with the *ber* spirit.

"Are you what I think you are?" Leyek asked.

Osborn steadied his shoulders.

The Blood Sorcerer's minion let out a delighted laugh. "You are. You're Ursan. A berserker, in fact. Thought we'd killed you all."

His fingers locked on the hilt of his sword. "You thought wrong."

Leyek flashed him a smile. "Good. Your women died crying and screaming, by the way. I'll enjoy your death just as much."

His berserkergang raged inside him, but Osborn tamped it down. He knew Leyek's words were lies and meant to provoke him.

Leyek made a show of examining the length of his nails. "Surprised you would be helping an Elden princess. Thought disguising our changeling vamps as those of Elden was a particularly clever bit of deception designed by my master. Although I will admit I did think the subtly of the ploy would be wasted on a beast."

A coldness crept into his body, and invaded his

chest. This wasn't the focusing chill of the berserkergang overtaking him—this was something different.

Kill.

Avenge.

Hurt.

Breena rested her soft hand on his shoulder. Quieting him.

His woman was right. This creature, this bearer of evil, wanted to anger him. Push him to make a mistake because this thing knew that, despite his command of blood magic, Osborn could still kill him. Would still kill him. With the power of his berserker ancestry and Breena's nearness.

Osborn raised his sword, calmly and with perfect balance.

Chapter 13

Every lesson, every word of caution and instruction, Osborn ever gave Breena now ran through her mind. She'd never been so afraid. She'd awoken not so long ago with only two commands echoing in her mind. To survive and to avenge.

Now she added a new one on her own: win this fight with Osborn.

Leyek raised his sword, waving it around in an elaborate dance.

It's the flourishing knights who are the first to die.

The air around her chilled. Osborn's berserkergang grew in strength. The Blood Sorcerer's minion charged. The clang of steel on steel rang through the air as Osborn blocked his blow. With an upswing of his sword, her warrior almost sent Leyek reeling to the floor.

She searched the crowd until she met Rolfe's eyes. Signaling toward the door, she mouthed the word, "Go!" With Leyek fully immersed in battle, now would be the time for her people to escape. With a nod, Rolfe silently gathered the Eldens who awaited their deadly fate and ushered them away.

With her people secure, Breena reached for her own sword. Two on one might not be a fair fight, but when did a wielder of blood magic deserve honor and respect?

Osborn charged forward, his sword slicing through his prey's shoulder. Leyek screeched at the pain, the sound horrible to hear; the walls began to shake, and dust rained down on their heads.

"That's the sound your vamps made as I killed them," Osborn shouted at him with a sneer. He thrust again, but Leyek was able to sidestep the blow.

The Blood Sorcerer's minion began to shake and mumble. Words, dark words, reverberated off the beams of the ceiling. A revolting menace permeated through the small hall. Nausea made her stomach roil.

"He's summoning his magic," she called.

Leyek moved in a flash. A slash appeared on the right side of Osborn's pelt. Then the left. With a gleeful cackle, the pelt fell to the floor and caught on fire.

Osborn's connection to the *ber* spirit was severed. Gone.

With a roar of outrage, Osborn rushed toward the minion. But some invisible force repelled him back, and left him bleeding. A nasty gash appeared across his chest, and blood seeped from the wound. Blood magic.

Osborn glanced down at his injury, and wiped across his ribs. His hand came back red with his blood. He stilled at the sight, and the room seemed to warm.

Then her warrior's face changed. The unrelenting rage lining his features softened. Replaced by determination. Osborn thrust, parried and thrust again.

Leyek stumbled backward, blood pouring from a gash across his face, and another wound to his side. Osborn charged once more, burying the blade in the minion's stomach. Leyek fell to the cold stone floor, his blood pooling around him.

"Tell me how they died again," Osborn ordered.

Leyek struggled to breathe. "I'll give you power. Great power. We'll bring the girl in together. My master will reward you greatly."

"Tell me how they died."

The minion's eyes turned the color of decay. He knew there'd be no ally in the Ursan standing over him. "I gave free rein to the vamps. Torture, devastate, torment… they did it all." Leyek's words began to slur, a murky haze surrounded him. The wound on his cheek began to heal. She would not let this thing live another day.

She ran to Osborn's side, and grabbed the steel of his sword. Breena gripped the blade so hard it cut into her flesh. Energy stirred within her, swirled and grew. With a snap it left her fingers, forging itself with the steel.

"My magic with your strength," Breena said. "It's time to finish him."

"It's only right," he answered.

Osborn steered her aside, kicked Leyek's blade toward him, then backed up. Her warrior eyed the Blood Sorcerer's minion. Waved him forward.

Leyek grabbed the hilt of his sword with bloody fingers. He chanted as he stood, but Breena no longer feared his brand of magic. He lunged at Osborn, and with only one strike from her warrior's sword, Leyek fell to the ground dead. Her magic had destroyed him.

Osborn wavered on his feet, and Breena ran toward him, looping his arm over her shoulders and helping him out the door. He needed to be in the fresh air, away from the death and magic of the blood.

"You did it, Osborn. And without your pelt."

"We did it together."

"You belong at my side, Breena," he told her once they'd crossed the threshold, loving the feel of her strength and trying to not let on that he was hurt as he appeared.

"Don't you mean you belong at *my* side?" she asked, a slow beautiful smile curving her lips.

"Yes." His breath flowed out as a relieved groan.

Her kissable lips turned pouty. "I was doing pretty well in there. You didn't have to turn all berserker."

"I am a berserker."

"Even without your pelt."

He nodded. The *ber* spirit would always be part of him. He understood that now. A lesson he could one day teach his brothers. "And yes, I did have to turn 'all berserker.' For you."

Breena stood on tiptoe and kissed his cheek. "That's why I love you. And him. Mostly you," she teased.

Osborn grabbed her hands. "You know I must go with you to Elden. The Blood Sorcerer killed my family, too."

Breena nodded. "I was hoping this was where you said you loved me, too."

She tried to pull her fingers from his grasp, but he wouldn't let go. He would never let go. "And I'm trying to tell you that I would have followed you to Elden, anyway. Even without knowing he was responsible for what happened to my people. I was returning to convince you, uh, that I belonged at your side when I heard the sound of your blade."

He let her hands drop. Her decision. Her choice.

She reached up and cupped his cheek, her thumb running along his lower lip.

"There will be another full moon tonight. Breena

of Elden, will you join me under the stars and seal your life with mine?"

After gripping his hands in her tiny ones, she gave his fingers a squeeze. "I don't know what we will face tomorrow, but tonight will be ours. Yes, Osborn."

"And, Breena?"

She gazed into his eyes. "Yes?"

"I love you."

Epilogue

The night of Leyek's defeat, Breena insisted they have a feast. She said it was in celebration, but Osborn knew she sensed her people needed festivity. The music, the dancing and the tales around the fire. To feel normal again. United as Eldens. The Blood Sorcerer had nearly broken them as a people. Truthfully many of them would never be the same, but tonight they would eat and laugh and forget.

Tomorrow would be for battle plans. Breena had already questioned every Elden in an attempt to ferret out news, even the most vague of rumors about her brothers. Osborn knew she'd never fully rest until she had her answers, even if they were tragic.

As the sun set, the fire blazed higher. By the hour more Eldens crept from the shadows to join her. Each one was greeted with laughter or tears and sometimes both. Families were re-united while others learned the knowledge of loved ones with stern acceptance. Grief would be for later. After the Blood Sorcerer's death.

As the stars filled the sky, Breena began to tell stories of Osborn's bravery, and the Eldens were thrilled to have a legendary Berserker join them in the upcoming battle. They laughed as she relayed his skills at dancing and he found himself smiling.

Osborn had hated these people of Elden for most of his life, wanted to annihilate them like his own people had been by the Blood Sorcerer. Now, for the first time in his life, Osborn found he was content. But not so content he didn't wonder how long they would be obligated to sit around the fire. He wanted nothing more than to draw Breena into the darkness of the night. To seal his life to hers as she'd promised. To lay his cloak on the ground and draw her down beside him and make love to her beneath the stars. He wanted nothing more than to hear her cries of pleasure.

Earlier today he'd thought he'd never see her

again, or hear her sweet voice again. Feel her touch. Sleep in his arms.

Rolfe moved to stand behind Breena. His steely gaze challenging as he crossed his arms over his chest. The message was clear. There'd be no sneaking away this night, or any night, until they were wed.

He gave the older warrior a nod of understanding, his intentions were honorable—marriage wise that was. What he wanted to do to Breena's body was wicked.

Even though their most dangerous days lay ahead of them, Osborn looked forward to the future. For the first time since he was a young boy of fifteen. Breena had given that to him.

Thankfully, Breena had moved away from stories of him and on toward tales of her training with the sword. Laughter settled around him, and he saw it took a moment for her people to wrap their minds around the changing image of her from sweet heir of Elden to warrior princess.

Two more men joined the circle around the fire, and he heard Breena gasp. His hand was instantly at his side, his fingers curling around the hilt of his sword.

Bernt and Torben stood there.

He raised to his feet. "How did—?"

Breena rushed to his brothers, kissing each

one on the cheek. "Magic. I left clues only they could follow."

Osborn didn't like the idea of them joining the fight, but they were almost men now. It was time he began accepting them that way. The Blood Sorcerer was responsible for taking away their childhood, and they had a right to the fight. His brothers settled around the fire, two more berserkers quickly welcomed. The people would entertain themselves long into the night.

"I can do more than just leave clues. I don't know if it's that I'm on Elden land again or that the battle with Leyek released something, but I can feel my power growing. Look."

Breena brought her hands together and he felt the change in her. Something powerful and elusive formed between her hands. Grew. Light pooled between her hands. "I can fully control my magic now. I don't have to rely on intense emotion."

His mind strayed to the intense emotion they'd used to mask the trace magic from the blood scouts at the lake and he nearly groaned.

The ball of light grew and she tossed it up into the air above her head where it separated into three distinct spheres. With a wave of her hand the spheres zipped across the sky, and he surveyed their progress until the light faded into the horizon. "I'm sending that out to my brothers."

A smile spread across her face. "I sense they are alive. I know it."

He'd been gifted with this incredible woman. He stay by her side until his last breath.

"The moon is full overhead," she whispered.

His heart pounded and his body hardened. In a few moments she'd be his forever. With a laugh, she lifted her skirts and took off at a run. "I'll be yours, but only if you catch me."

Osborn was too quick for her and reached for her hands. "Just try to get away."

Like most little girls, Breena had often dreamed of her wedding day. She'd wear a stunning dress, formal and beaded with a long train the colors of Elden. Her husband would, of course, be courtly and handsome, and he'd take her to his palace after the wedding feast and the dancing.

Never once had she expected the man who'd one day be her husband would be more inclined to growl than to dance. And tonight, she wore the sage dress her future husband had bought for her, the golden snake armband securely in place. Better than any imagined wedding finery.

Instead of a great hall filled with a long list of aristocratic and highborn guests to view the royal proceedings, they walked hand in hand, just the two of them, surrounded by the trees and under a canopy of stars. The reality of Osborn was more perfect than anything she'd ever dreamed or imagined.

Osborn, her wild berserker of a man, loved her.

Once they'd reached a small clearing, he stopped and turned toward her, twining his fingers with hers.

Glancing up, she gasped when she saw his appearance. "What happened to your hair?" she asked. All of Osborn's long brown locks were gone, his hair cut close to his head.

"Another tradition of my people. On his wedding day, a man cuts his hair. A taming, if you will."

Breena laughed. She doubted there would be much taming where this man was concerned. His new look would take a little getting used to, but she liked it.

The lines crinkling at the corners of his eyes smoothed, and his expression turned serious. "Breena, my love. I seal my life with yours."

Such simple words. No elaborate vows or flourishes. Just a man taking the woman he wanted out into nature and declaring himself as hers before the stars and under the moon. A swell of love and emotion made her eyes tear. But she would not cry. Her warrior deserved a warrioress.

"Osborn, my love," she told him in a clear, strong voice. She met his brown eyes and smiled. "I seal my life with yours."

* * *

Once upon a time there was a beautiful princess who only really lived when she dreamed. Then one day she woke up surrounded by three glowering bears. With patience and love she tamed the fiercest, and with a kiss transformed the beast into a prince.

* * * * *

Special Offers

Every month we put together collections and longer reads written by your favourite authors.

Here are some of next month's highlights—and don't miss our fabulous discount online!

On sale 18th November

On sale 18th November

On sale 18th November

Find out more at
www.millsandboon.co.uk/specialreleases

Visit us Online

1211/ST/MB352